# PIRATE QUEEN

## BOOK OF THE NAVIGATOR

## H. N. KLETT

RAVEN ROCK PRESS

Pirate Queen:
Book of the Navigator
H.N. Klett

This is a work of fiction. Any resemblance to actual persons living or dead, businesses, events or locales is purely coincidental. Reproduction in whole or part of this publication without express written consent is strictly prohibited.

Pirate Queen: Book of the Navigator
Copyright © 2017 by H.N. Klett.



Published by: Raven Rock Press
Edited by: Crystal Watanabe
Typeset by: Jay Artale
Cover Design by: M. Wayne Miller

Library of Congress Control Number: 2016954706
ISBN 978-0-9979699-0-0 print
ISBN 978-0-9979699-1-7 mobi
ISBN 978-0-9979699-2-4 epub
ISBN 978-0-9979699-3-1 PDF
ISBN 978-0-9979699-4-8 Audiobook
10 9 8 7 6 5 4 3 2 1
First edition, 2017

Young adult fiction: Adventure YAF001010, YAF001000
Young adult fiction: fantasy YAF019000
Young adult fiction: science fiction YAF056000

Raven Rock Press
P.O.Box 284
Browns Summit, NC 27214

Visit:
hnklett.com

*To my family and friends.*
*You all told me I could.*
*You were right.*
*HNK*

# PRELUDE

Captain Seamus Pike felt ill at ease looking out at the wall of mist approaching them. When he looked at it, he swore it was looking back at him. He wondered what the crew would have made of this portent, had they been up. His crew looked for signs of ill omens in everything. Ill omens in the birds in the air, the schools of fish in the water, even the amount of foam that was in their mugs of grog could be an ill omen. Seamus didn't believe any of it, but the heavy mists of the evening raised the fine hairs on the back of his neck.

Their sloop, the *Polly*, was anchored off the tropical island of Vregora, just outside of the trader's port of Baron's Bay. The island's climate was known to be steamy and sometimes unbearable, but much calmer than the weeks of cold wet winds and rough waters they had just endured to get there.

They rested just off the shore, away from the traffic lanes, where the warm tropical waters sometimes met with the cool currents from the north. It wasn't the presence of mists that bothered him—mists could be found anywhere in the world; there was even a large Sea of Mists to the far north, not that he ever risked going through it—the unusual thickness of these mists just didn't seem natural to Seamus. As a lifelong sailor, he had grown up skirting the mists, but these were somehow different.

He sat quietly and watched as they continued to creep in. It was like some sort of sea beast silently approaching, intent on consuming the ship and its sleeping crewmen one bite at a time. Seamus was the only one awake to witness it. He had chosen to man the night's watch alone.

He had been all too happy to let both shifts of crew get a full night of rest, since he would benefit from it in the end with the crew's hardiness and good will, something he needed for the four-week haul back to their home port of Jakar in the north. A rested crew meant a better sailing crew. Seamus decided that the cost of loneliness for the night would be worth the price of taking the lone watch and getting home to his family sooner. But now, looking over the mists, he felt a slight chill and questioned the wisdom of his decision.

The mists reminded Seamus of stories his father had told him and his brothers when they were children—tales of spirits in the mists, ghost pirates out on the seas, searching for souls to join their crew.

As the plumes of fog slowly crept over the rails and coated the deck, Seamus remembered his father's warning about misty waters:

> Eyes of red
> of the pirate dead
> Are on the hunt for you.
> Beware the mists,
> And take no risks,
> Lest you become a ghost pirate, too.

A jolt of cold fear sliced into his spine like a scalpel. His eyes tried to focus on the mists that had now entirely enveloped their ship, but it was just a solid wall of gray that revealed little and covered everything.

The heavy trod of boots came from behind him. Seamus spun around to track the noise and quickly found himself caught in the glare of a pair of glowing red eyes that beamed through the mists at him. Those eyes began to approach him.

Seamus froze, a scream firmly wedged in his throat. He found it hard to breathe.

The large and imposing figure stopped just a short distance away from him, its glowing ruby eyes unblinking as they stared at him. With a gloved hand, it drew a dark and sinister cutlass from a worn and moldy sheath and pointed it at Seamus's chest.

"W-w-what is it you want?" Seamus gagged on the words.

The figure stood there, unnaturally still.

Seamus's gaze kept moving back and forth from the cutlass to the glowing red eyes that stared at him, unblinking. His frantic mind clawed at him like a cat trying to escape drowning. Whatever this thing wanted, he would give, just to make it go away. But what did it want?

It leaned towards him. Its jaw did not move when it spoke.

"*The book*," said the figure.

Silence.

There could only be one book they were after: the book with the skull on it. It was a book that couldn't be opened.

"I-I-I don't have it."

The figure cocked its head, its ghostly visage impossibly menacing as it stood there, its glowing eyes searching him.

Most books written by someone other than the Crown or Church were deemed subversive and marked as contraband. To have one was considered to be a hangable offense. In certain sailing circles, it was known that Seamus was a collector of some of those rare and outlawed books that bought you a ticket to the long drop with the short stop by the hangman's noose.

Another pair of glowing red eyes appeared beside the captain, and stared at Seamus, unblinking. The two never turned their gaze from Seamus as the first figure addressed the other set of eyes. It gave only one command, the lightly spoken words drifting through the mist.

"SEARCH THE SHIP."

OUT OF THE mists blossomed a multitude of red glowing eyes inside of dark human-like forms, which then washed over the decks. Seamus numbly turned and watched as the flood of ghostly forms swept down into the bowels of the ship, where the crew slept unaware. There were no screams from a surprised crew, only the sound of rushing boots above and below decks.

Turning back to his captor, Seamus looked over the creature, still stoically standing impossibly still and holding him at bay with its icy gaze. The creature's clothes looked old and threadbare. The once bright red seaman's coat was dark and mottled with age, its edges frayed by use. Its dark captain's hat was rimmed with mold and was in the shape and style of a time long ago. The tangles of dark hair that fell about its shoulders looked like thick ropes of seaweed and framed the fearsome and glowing features of its skull. The moist, moldy scent of the monstrous creature clawed its way into Seamus's nose and at his sanity.

"I don't have it! I swear!" Seamus gasped at the figure, still trying to catch his breath.

After a few minutes, footsteps sounded behind Seamus, and joining them to his right stood another towering ghost pirate with glowing red eyes and a gruesome-looking hook for a left hand.

In a deep and gravelly voice, it said, "He speaks the truth. It's not here."

Seamus turned back to the ghost pirate captain and shrilled like a child, "I told you I don't have it! I traded it to another merchant in Baron's Bay."

"*WHO?*" the ghost captain bellowed. The question boomed into Seamus like a cannon shot. The ghost captain leaned closer to him and cocked its head slightly.

If this was the only way he could get rid of them, then Seamus would do it. His head was dizzy, and he felt his knees starting to give way. There was an odd chemical taste in his mouth and his eyes wouldn't stop watering. His face went numb and the world grew dark as the words dripped from his mouth.

"His name is Orin Heartstone... h-h-he's the captain of the *Arrow*."

# CHAPTER 1

Many miles to the northeast, Orin Heartstone's ship, the *Arrow*, raced the dawn. Low-slung and lean with two great masts brimming over with brightly colored sails, it grabbed the winds in a burst of splendor matching the dawn. Its sleek and light wooden hull leaned into the water like a racing sloop. At full sail, the vessel almost skipped over the water like a cannon shot.

The *Arrow* was the fastest merchant vessel in the western hemisphere and the pride of her home port of Daden, and it ranged the globe flying Daden's colors of green and gold in sail and flag. The *Arrow* could outrun anything.

Normally there was no need to rush their return, but they were at full sail and barreling on towards home. The few days they had spent in the port of Baron's Bay had been incredibly profitable. They weren't due to return home for several more days, but Orin's mother had sent him a dispatch at port. It said to hurry home and nothing more. Dispatches over great distances were an incredible rarity and wildly expensive. Orin's mother may have been a lot of things, but loose with money was not one of them. She had never sent a dispatch before.

Orin tried not to let worry get the better of him. As he often told his daughter, Hailey, there was no point worrying about things you couldn't control, and the only thing a good captain could have control over was the present moment. Hailey would have been a fine captain, if only she wasn't a girl.

Hailey had a keen, discerning eye and a sharp wit, but often held her tongue, sometimes to her detriment. t She could be bold, however, when she felt she was allowed to be. She had grown up on the *Arrow* as the daughter of a merchant sea captain. She knew everything there was to know about sailing and running an efficient ship. She could tie down a mainsail before she could tie her shoes. Not only did she know seven different ways to rig a ship, she could instruct you on each one of them. She was a talent at sea, but her true calling was navigation.

Before Hailey had become a teenager, she had full run of the ship, helping where she could. Every night Orin would sit her down over hot chocolate and show her the maps and weather tools, teaching her the ways of navigation. He taught her to navigate anywhere—where they were, where they needed to go, and why they chose the route they did.

He taught her how to use the devices and magical tools leased to them by the Crown. She became adept with the contraption that predicted the weather hours in advance, but using the compass and navigational charts were her true loves.

It got to the point that Orin finally conceded that she was a natural and made her unofficial navigator of the ship. As she grew older, though, Orin started listening to her counsel less and less when it came to navigating. He stopped listening to her at all, really. She was no longer his little girl.

As Orin's mother often reminded him, Hailey was a young lady now and shouldn't dirty her hands with such work. It was unseemly for a woman to learn the craft of sailing. Even more so for a young woman to be around a crew of sailors.

He wrinkled his brow when it occurred to him that it was she who had plotted this quicker course home. It was the last act of navigation he could allow. She had skillfully plotted and replotted a course that narrowly dodged a large storm he missed that would have slowed them immensely had they run into it or tried to wait it out. The rosy dawn before him was their reward for narrowly missing the rains. He stood and appreciated it for a moment, as the last stars of the night disappeared into the rising light. He looked up from the quarterdeck and knew exactly where to find her.

He could barely see her at the top of the main sail, but she was there and completely unaware that this was the last time she would be able to climb such heights with him.

Hailey leaned against the spar while balancing on the footropes, her hands quickly working the sextant to line up on the few stars twinkling in the morning twilight. Satisfied, she set it back into her pouch and found herself lost in her commanding view of the beautiful world of Ephryae. It stretched out before her like a treasure chest overturned. Its sapphire-blue waters spilled out to the horizon and crashed into the wrinkle of deep-emerald land on the horizon under a garnet-colored dawn. At that moment, she felt like the richest person in the world.

From below, she heard her father's voice call out to her.

"Hailey! I took the celestial fix earlier this morning. Come down."

She let out the exasperated sigh of a teenager and pulled

the notebook out from under her arm, made a note, then made her way down the rope ladder and to Orin on the quarterdeck. His eyes followed her progression down the rigging.

Hailey's single braid bobbed back and forth on her shoulders as she easily worked her way down the ropes. Her dark brown hair was woven with several light streaks running from the crown of her head, bleached by the sun. The dark and light contrasted and complemented one another as they were woven into the braid. Like her father's hair, it was a sign that she was a girl from the isle of Arwend.

She wore an outfit that was a step above pajamas, but only slightly. A comfortably loose shirt and baggy short pants that came to just above the knee were fine for crawling around a ship, but as Orin's mother constantly reminded them both, it wasn't proper for a young lady to crawl around a ship. In his head, Orin could hear his mother clucking like a mad hen at him about it. They would be at port soon, and he knew she was waiting. So did Hailey.

Hailey wasn't a little girl anymore, even though she still dressed like one. She had grown as tall and beautiful as her mother Rebecca once was, though her hair was different. Her mother's hair had been long and as black as a raven's wing. It had flowed past her shoulders and down to the small of her back, much like most of the people of her home on the far away isle of Iconen. Despite the minor difference, Orin found himself looking at Hailey from time to time with a touch of sadness. For just a moment, he would catch a glimpse of his late wife in her smile.

He wished that Rebecca could have seen Hailey now. Hailey might not be a proper lady according to his mother, but she was smart and beautiful, and he was proud of how wonderfully she had turned out. He only wished that life could have stayed as it was back when Rebecca was alive. Life had changed so much since she died.

When Orin had received the news of his beloved Rebecca's death, he'd been devastated. For a time, he had simply shut down. It was if he weren't there anymore, just a shell of a man standing around, waiting for the world to stop along with him. He wouldn't eat, wouldn't sleep, wouldn't do anything. Orin's mother, Rose, had moved in not only to take care of him but also to help raise Hailey.

Grandmother Rose became the dominant force in their household during Orin's temporary absence. For a time, it seemed to Hailey that she had lost both of her parents. She wasn't sure which was worse, the complete absence of her mother from her life or the presence of the shell of her father as he wasted away. She worked as hard as she could to help bring him back.

When Orin finally started to come around, it was as if he had been asleep for a long time. Right away, he started to notice a few things he didn't like, such as the way his mother harassed Hailey about courtly manners and the expectations of women. Still, he said nothing and watched his daughter wriggle under the strain. He was too weak emotionally to fight with his mother. His heart was too damaged from losing Rebecca, and the shame of his shutting down was too great to allow him to say anything.

Grandmother Rose felt it was her duty and obligation to see to it that Hailey was "properly educated," now that her mother wasn't around. After moving in, she forced Hailey to adopt an entirely new way of living. Her grandmother called it the life of a proper young lady.

Her life went from one of adventure on the high seas to one of dull and mind-numbing propriety. She was forced into formal dress attire, endless tea parties, manners classes, elocution lessons, not to mention the endless reading of dry materials from a primer that told her every way to do, be, and think.

When Orin finally objected, Grandmother Rose tersely explained to him that, though he was a wonderful father to Hailey, he was still only a man. He could never understand the social ways of women and the importance of Hailey's being properly trained.

According to Rose, the loss of Hailey's mother had not only hurt the child emotionally, it hurt her socially. In a society where the only advancement a woman had was determined through social circles, Hailey was already at a disadvantage learning so late in life. Such a late start meant she would not be able to climb the social ladder high enough and fast enough to marry a noble, the end goal for any young lady. She could be forced to settle for a commoner and hope that he could support her and any children they had. Rose intended to make up that difference quickly by shoving Hailey up the social ladder. She would bring her to the pinnacle of ladyship, whether Orin and Hailey liked it or not.

And Hailey did not.

Hailey padded over to him in her bare feet.

"What is it, Dad?"

"Now, daughter, is that how your Grandmother Rose taught you to greet your elders?" He gave her a wry smile and scratched at the stubble of a few days' growth on his face.

She wrinkled her nose, mocked a curtsey, and said in an overly flowery voice, "I'm sorry, dearest Papa. How may I serve you?" Her high cheeks glowed bright with mischief.

"Better." Orin mockingly gave a bow and a big toothy grin in return. "You know you shouldn't be climbing around the rigging. You know what your grandmother would say."

"It's no place for a lady," they both said.

"But it's the only place I could get an accurate sighting..."

She felt herself whining and hated it. She sounded like a little girl.

"You need to start listening to your grandmother. She knows best. Ladies don't climb rigging."

Exasperated, she let out another long sigh.

"Then how am I supposed to take the readings?"

"I told you, I already did them this morning."

Hailey wanted to tell him her readings were always more accurate than his, but he knew it, so she thought better of it. Her father was a proud sailor, and a good one. She wasn't sure how he'd react if she corrected him publicly. It was bad enough to be insubordinate to the captain of a merchant ship, but for a woman to do it might cause more trouble than she could handle. Grandmother Rose's lessons had taught her as much.

She looked down at the deck in surrender.

He took her by the shoulders. "Look, I know you love navigation, and you are good at it, but I can't have you doing it anymore."

"But..." she stammered, "if I'm good at it, why not let me?"

"Because you are a young lady now. Climbing around the rigging and playing with charts is no job for a young woman. That's not how things are. You are supposed to either enjoy the view on the deck or stay in a cabin and out of the way. That is what everyone expects. That is what your grand-mother expects."

She shook off his grip and looked at him defiantly.

"It's not what Mom would have expected."

The towering man's face went dark, and the once kind eyes flashed like thunderbolts. She was right, and he knew it, which made him all the angrier. Rebecca had been her own free spirit and did as she pleased, thumbing her nose at what was proper or not. It was one of the many things that he'd loved about her and that his mother had hated, and she reminded him of that every chance she could.

He glanced around the deck to see if any of the men had taken notice of their exchange. If they had, they didn't show it and went about their business either swabbing the deck, carrying supplies around, or working the rigging.

"Look, Hailey," he said with a sigh and ran a hand over his pulled-back hair, "your mother is gone, and there's nothing we can do about it. I want to make sure you are taken care of, and this is how we do it." He placed a large hand on her shoulder and tilted his head, imploring her. "Your grandmother is doing her best to raise you the right way. The proper way a young lady should be raised. It's the only way you will be able to fit in and someday find a man who can take care of you."

"Why can't you take care of me?"

"Because I won't always be around! Neither will your grandmother."

"Then why can't I just take care of myself without a—"

"That's enough!" he barked.

Out of the corner of her eye, Hailey saw two sailors flinch.

He ran both hands over the top of his head and held his breath for a moment. Then he released it, sounding like a teakettle hissing as he let his arms drop to his sides. He could scream and fight with the crew all he wanted, but his daughter was an altogether different matter.

He looked at her with exasperation and frustration. Through gritted teeth he said, "Hailey, that's not how things work..."

She stared at him blankly. She couldn't understand what had happened, what had changed in everyone's mind once she became a teenager. When she was younger she'd had free rein to learn and do as she pleased, and Dad was never this distant with her. She could explore the ship, do things to help out, get dirty with the crew. She would sneak around and read any book she found, even the secret banned ones her father hid and collected, which were vibrant and full of knowledge and wonder.

Every evening the two of them would get together and talk about all she had done and learned, and he would delight in her achievements. Her future had seemed as open as the view of the horizon from the top mast. But as she got older, her view shrank more and more every day. She could no longer explore or get dirty. The things they gave her to read and learn from now were dry, dull, and uninteresting propaganda from the Church of the Ancients that told her what to do and how to act. Her father had stopped asking her about what she had learned and had been spending less and less time with her. The once great horizon she had seen became a small porthole through which she could barely see anymore. A framed portrait of a young lady for some man to own one day.

Orin turned and paced about in a short circle to calm himself, to get his bearings. He reminded Hailey of a spoon swirling milk into a cup of tea. It had the same calming effect.

After calming himself after several turns, Orin finally stopped and rounded on her.

"We should be back in port by noon. Have you read that primer your grandmother gave you?"

Hailey sighed and deflated, slumping her shoulders forward, and began a whine that Orin quickly silenced by holding up a meaty hand.

"Look, Hailey, she's doing this to help you. You need to read it."

Hailey snorted.

"Come on now, you promised." He paused and changed

tactics. "You do know it will be me that she will go after if you haven't done your reading, right?"

She did, and he knew Hailey hated how her grandmother went after him. Grandmother Rose was like a furious hen, constantly harassing and pecking away at him till her dad gave in to whatever she wanted. If Hailey didn't read the primer, Grandmother Rose would be all over him the second he got off the boat, all claws and feathers. She couldn't let her do that to him.

But Hailey decided that if she was going to give in, she was going to make a show of it. She sighed dramatically.

"Fine." She folded her arms and looked off over the rail.

Orin smiled and said, "That's a good girl." He waved over his first mate, Rufus, who had been unsuccessfully trying to ignore their conversation as he worked.

Rufus Sprada was a tall, thin, and wiry man with dark, angled features that reminded Hailey of a snake, and she trusted him just as much as one. Whether it was his odd appearance his narrow eyes that were always on her, she never liked being around him. He gave her the creeps.

"Rufus, could you take the young lady to my cabin to make sure she reads her primer?"

The first mate fixed Hailey with a smile that she swore had fangs. Most people annoyed Rufus simply by their existence, but children like Hailey annoyed him even more. She knew he felt that she got underfoot and slowed up work, and work was everything to the man. Ever since she was little, he was always the first one to look for an excuse to get her out of the way.

"Gladly, sir." He winked at her.

Hailey glared at her father, but he shrugged in reply.

"Sorry, Hailey, but a promise is a promise."

Hailey didn't look back as Rufus escorted her the short walk off the quarterdeck to the captain's cabin. Rufus opened the door, did a mock bow to her, and pushed her in. As he shut the door, he grinned his serpent smile at her and said, "Have fun reading your book!"

She heard him chuckle as he leaned against the door, standing guard. To Hailey, it was apparent that the situation mirrored her life: forcefully shoved into a place she didn't want to go, to do something she didn't want to do, and trapped with no way out.

# CHAPTER 2

*H*ailey looked around the cabin and saw it was the same sparse wooden box it had always been. Space on any vessel was at a premium, especially in the captain's quarters. Though most of the crew had only hammocks and fourteen feet apiece below decks, the captain was afforded a small room with a trundle bed.

Until recently, her cot lay beside it, now removed. Her father had moved her to her own private hammock below, separate from the crew, on this trip. When asked why, he only told her that a young lady needed her space. She thought this ironic because, even though this cabin was sparse, it had far more room than the space she had been allotted below.

She walked past the simple wooden table, behind which sat the captain's chair, and made her way to the pictures that hung on the walls. It was an uncommon luxury to hang a picture on any wall of a ship. Due to the sea's rolling nature, it took work to keep them there. Captains didn't usually waste time on such things. They had ships to run, crews to keep in line. The last thing they wanted to bother with was decoration. Her father was different, though. He'd spent so much of his life on the sea since her mother died, he started to make what once was a temporary cabin into a home. Little by little, he was rebuilding his life -- the life of a man whose home was the sea.

Inspecting each piece, Hailey wasn't sure if the nails holding the battered frames to the wall of the cabin did more to hold the frames together than hang them up.

There were three paintings that hung on the wall. The first was a painting of the *Arrow* at port; her mother had painted it years ago. The second was a framed map showing their home shores of Daden. The third was the most special of all. It was different. Compared to the other two, it was much more carefully cared for. It was a portrait of her mother. Her mother Rebecca had died three years ago when Hailey was twelve, old enough that she could remember her, and for that she was thankful. Looking at her portrait, Hailey couldn't help but notice in the reflection of the glass how much she had started to look like her.

Hailey reached her arms out to the portrait of her mother, feeling the frame, its painted wood smooth under her fingers. She felt along the right side for the familiar spot she had found many years ago. There was a small click, and the portrait swung aside on hinges like a cabinet door to reveal a hidden compartment with a lock on it.

Like all merchant ships, there were several hidden compartments in which to smuggle contraband. This one in particular held the most valuable contraband in the world, at least to her. She pulled a pin out of her hair and set to work on the lock.

She had been an especially curious child. She knew that her father and mother made a habit of collecting and keeping banned books, and being a voracious reader like her mother, she longed to read them.

One day her father caught her trying to get her hands on the books behind the portrait. After that he installed the locked door on his secret cabinet. He promised that she would one day read the books that they had collected, but only when she was older and mature enough. Of course, being restricted from them only meant her need to understand what was in them grew stronger. Why had the Queen outlawed them? She had to find out.

Hailey had learned to pick locks from one of the shiftier transient crewmen who had sailed with them for a few years. She was a fast learner and quickly gained access to the books on her own, mostly while her father was working on deck or away in town trading and possibly acquiring more rare books. She suspected her father knew of her little invasions, though he never directly mentioned it. When her grandmother came to live with them, he became quiet about the private library. Grandmother did not approve.

Hailey worked the lock with her hairpin, gently feeling the pins slide into place. The door sprang open with a slight pinging sound, and there before her were the leather-bound books she had grown to love. She knew each one of them by heart. Stories about the colonial rebellion against the Crown, passionate treatises on the reasons the colonies should be independent, the histories of the first cities and the grand council that later gave way to the monarchy; it was all there. Her eyes lit over each leather-bound volume as if she were a mother duck counting her ducklings to see if all were accounted for.

She grinned widely as she spotted a book she had never seen before on the end. Her dad had disappeared a long time when they were at the port in Baron's Bay. Usually his hunts for new books didn't last long. This one had taken most of the day, and when he returned, he looked worn down and tired. Looking over the elaborate binding of the book, she could tell that he'd traded many a favor to get it. Sliding it out from the cabinet, she held it and admired the craftsmanship.

Bookmaking was truly an artisan's craft, and this one was an amazing prize. The journal, only slightly larger than her hand, was wrapped in rich red leather that was soft to the touch despite the hard spine. What was curious was the ornateness of it. A woven knot of silver inlay adorned the cover and was punctuated by a silver skull with two dark ruby eyes. Protruding from under the woven knot and skull, metal bands stretched out and wrapped around the book, keeping it firmly closed.

She shut the cabinet, swung the painting back in place, and made her way behind the desk to admire the book more closely in the light coming through the windows. This book was a puzzle to her, unlike all the others, for it was locked. She had to find a way to get into it. She turned it over in her hands, looking for clues on how to open it.

She knew one thing, at least. The skull on the cover told her right away that this book had something to do with the mythology of the phantom pirates that were only spoken of in hushed tones. You didn't have to be a merchant's daughter to hear about the ghost pirates; just live by the sea, and you'd hear any number of tales. Many sightings of their ghostly black ships were rumored from port to port, despite how much the Crown or the Church denied they ever existed. They were said to be the souls of sailors and explorers lost at sea, searching the world for more crew and more treasure.

Perhaps once, there were pirates, long ago, but with the iron fist of the Crown, no one would dare think of such a thing today. Truth or fiction, there were plenty of stories about them, most riddled with skeleton captains and crews staring at you from skulls with fiery eyes and the treasure and plunder they would take from unwary vessels ensnared in their creeping mists.

The only ghost that Hailey knew about was the void that was left in the world when her mother died. Her absence haunted Hailey and her father on a daily basis. Hailey would have traded a thousand pirate treasures just to have her back.

Again and again she turned over the book, and it would not yield its secrets to her. She could see that there was no visible way to open the book. There was no keyhole, no release latch -- it was all smooth metal. The bands wrapped around the book to a design on the back cover and dove into the metal work of the emblem on the front cover. She traced her finger around the knotted design surrounding the skull, hoping to find something. She thought maybe there was a trick to the skull and its weird red eyes. She pushed on the ruby stones, thinking that it might pop open to reveal a keyhole or something, but instead she felt a slight pinch, and her finger began to bleed.

"Ow!" she exclaimed, more out of surprise than pain. There must have been a rough piece she cut her finger on, though the stones appeared too smooth to have cut her finger like that.

She set the book down on the barren table and stuck her finger in her mouth. The eyes of the skull looked different to her somehow, as though there was a slight red glow to them, but she dismissed it as a trick of lighting. But then the straps on the book popped open with a sound she could have sworn was a sigh, and she jumped slightly.

The fine hair on the back of Hailey's neck began to stand up, and the air felt charged, static. She stepped forward, finger still in her mouth. The skull on the book watched her with its smooth, simmering ruby eyes. She reached out to the cover and pulled it open to reveal...

nothing.

She flipped the pages. One after the other was blank and unremarkable. Hailey couldn't help but feel cheated. She wondered if it was just a sketchbook or something. But if that were the case, why the ornate cover and lock?

The pages felt odd to the touch, as if they were made of a fine cloth material, not paper. She had just placed her hand on the page to feel its texture, when the book sprang to life.

Words bubbled to the surface of the page like oil erupting from the ground. Words and images began to run across the page, racing to fill it. Hailey picked up the book excitedly. When she did, a large ornate map appeared and hung in the air before her.

She could see the whole of Ephryae. She could see the tropical continent of Vregora, whose port of Baron's Bay they had departed just days ago. She could see her home port of Daden, nestled in the island of Arwend, jutting out off to the southeast. All the smaller islands like Aibronne, Iconen, Eolan, Agoth, and even the tiny Eyica islands off the coast of the largest landmass of Phesin: They were all there floating in the air before her. Small arrows danced over the map, indicating wind and weather fronts. Little flags denoted names of ports, and there were even tiny markers showing boats, including the *Arrow* itself.

Looking more closely at the tiny image of their ship, she could see not only the direction they were going, she could see the speed and the time when they would arrive at port based on their present course. She would have remained transfixed on the living image before her, if she hadn't noticed the book. She watched as pages changed from bright white to solid black to bright white over and over again, only stopping when she gave the book her full attention. Then it cleared to a blank page.

Then urgent words were quickly bubbling up on the page. Hailey read:

*HAILEY, YOU ARE IN GREAT DANGER! YOU MUST*
*HIDE ME!*

"What?" she found herself asking the empty room. How did this thing know her name?

The page cleared and new words appeared on the page.

**OF COURSE I KNOW YOUR NAME, HAILEY!**
**I SAID, YOU ARE IN GREAT DANGER!**
**NAVIGATOR.**
**THEY WILL COME FOR YOU.**

Was this book really talking to her? It was starting to scare her. Hailey tried to control her breathing.

"What? Who is coming to get me?"

The page cleared again and the words were replaced.

**THE PIRATES**
**THEY NEED THEIR NAVIGATOR**
**THEY WILL COME FOR YOU.**

Her mind raced with her pulse. Pirates? Pirates aren't real. They were just made-up ghouls from children's and sailors' stories, weren't they? Why her? Why do they even want her as a navigator?

No, this couldn't be real. This couldn't be happening. She felt pale, and a cold sweat, like icy hands, trickled down her neck and back.

The page cleared, and new words appeared on the page.

**THIS IS REAL**
**DON'T LET ME FALL INTO THE HANDS**
**OF THE CROWN!**
**DON'T WORRY, THE PIRATES ARE COMING FOR YOU.**

Don't worry? Hailey slammed the book shut in her hand. She wanted nothing more to do with this thing. Its bands reattached with a mechanical click. She had to put it back.

There were the sounds of boots by the door and someone fumbling with keys. Hailey had to think fast. She glanced at the portrait to make sure it was closed and stuffed the book in the waistband of her pants. She barely got it covered with her shirt before her father entered the cabin. She turned to face him.

He looked at her for a long moment.

"What's wrong with you, girl? You look as though you've just seen a ghost."

A ghost? Did he know? She wanted to confess, to tell him that she had found the book and that it started talking to her, showing her things, and telling her that she is the Navigator and that the pirates were coming to get her...but she couldn't. If she told him, it would have meant she knew how to get into the secret cabinet, and she would never see those books again.

"What? No. You just startled me, that's all."

She brought her breathing under control as he feigned interest in looking around the room. Hailey knew right away he was trying to hide the fact that he was looking to see if his secret compartment had been disturbed.

Satisfied that it hadn't, he turned to her and folded his arms.

"I thought you were supposed to be reading your primer?"

The weight of the book in her waistband reminded her of her guilt, but she smoothed her shirt and decided to play it off.

"I was, but I guess I just got lost in thought."

She crossed the room, reached into the bag that lay on the floor, and fished out the copy of the Church's primer her grandmother had packed for her. When anyone came of age, they received a copy, usually from the clergy or a relative. It contained in long and gloriously dull detail all the rules and etiquette of life as dictated by the Book of the Ancestors. It had been taught for years, but ever since the Queen ascended to the throne when Hailey was little, each passing year saw those rules enforced more and more.

She held it up to him as proof, then padded across the cabin back to the table and chair and placed the book on the table. The weight and size of the hidden book made it awkward to sit down, but her father didn't notice.

Though she dreaded reading the boring and vacuous book, she was relieved to find that the words did not change or try to talk to her like the last one.

Satisfied, Orin turned to go, but Rufus was standing in the doorway.

"Sir? There's a ship moving quickly toward us. It's hailing us. It looks to be a Crown ship."

The captain scowled as someone on deck shouted for all hands.

# CHAPTER 3

On deck, they could see that the large Crown ship, the *Vigilant*, was already upon them and turning alongside. The *Arrow* had struck her sails and floated patiently as the large ship glided up to them.

Looking over at the ship, Hailey noted that their sails looked completely different from any she had ever seen. They looked darker and more conical, like arrowheads instead of the tall, square sails she was accustomed to. She had heard that Crown ships were full of all kinds of magic, like lights without wicks or candles, and their navigators had the ability to predict the weather days in advance. Their ships were floating troves of magic items from the Queen that defied comprehension.

The *Vigilant*, sitting taller in the water than the low and lean-slung *Arrow*, extended a gangway down to their deck, and a detachment of marines boarded the ship without a word. They filed to the end of the gangway and then, forming two rows, stood at attention.

From the top of the gangway, a portly figure dressed in the red royal uniform of a Crown captain addressed Orin.

"Permission to come aboard?"

He didn't look so much at Orin as in his general direction.

"Please," Orin replied, knowing that there was no question in this man's asking, just a statement of formality. Orin knew that since that ship beside them was the *Vigilant*, then he would have to be cautious. Its captain, Captain Langen, had a reputation of being a man you wouldn't want to trifle with.

The marine detachment parted, allowing the captain down the plank.

The captain waddled down the plank and extended a hand to Orin, who took it carefully, like a stray dog taking a treat from a stranger. He was trying to figure out if he was about to be rewarded or taken and stewed.

Orin gave him his brightest smile. "To what do we owe the pleasure, sir?"

Hailey knew that her father had absolutely no love for the Crown or any of the Queen's representatives, especially after all they had put him through. She also knew that her father wouldn't be so foolish as to display any distaste for them. Any insult could lead to their staring down the barrels of an eighty-gun warship or dangling from the end of a noose. The Crown was not known for its tolerance.

"Searching for contraband, I'm afraid. Shouldn't take long."

The captain raised his chubby hand to the sergeant of the marine detachment, and they all spread out and began scour the ship.

"Be so good as to make sure that all of your crew stays on deck, please. I wouldn't want to" —he paused, and his cherub-like jocularity vanished, replaced by a look of menace, and then quickly changed back to his smiling demeanor— "cause you any further delay."

The effect wasn't just chilling for Orin; all crewmen within earshot behind Orin realized their lives were in very real danger should they not comply.

The marines climbed all over the ship as the crew stood waiting. The captain and Orin chatted to pass the time. The rest of the crew muttered amongst themselves, very aware of the many eyes lining the railings of the *Vigilant,* looking down on them. Hailey walked closer to the railing of the *Arrow* to get a look at them and noticed that each soldier had a long rifle resting at his side. That is, everyone with the exception of a rather tall, dapper gentleman dressed in a deep blue coat and pants, both accented with gold. He was looking down on them, seemingly amused.

She caught his eye, and he gave her a wide smile, then reached up with his long, spindly arms and tipped his perfectly matching hat, its blue-and-green feather fluttering in the breeze. Hailey didn't know why, but she suddenly felt a chill and shuddered.

She knew that this must be someone important, someone who had enough wealth to wear the latest fashions of the capital city of Davos. His bark-brown hair showed as much and was nicely combed and parted. Even at that distance she could tell his face was a slightly lighter tan than everyone else who spent their days in the sun. Even odder still, he was freshly shaven.

There was a reason most sailors wore beards. It's not an easy feat to swipe a blade across the face without drawing blood on any sized ship at the mercy of the rolling sea. Studying his angular features, she surmised that whoever worked a blade across his face must have an unbelievable amount of skill.

This was no man to be rude to, though she didn't want to linger in his attention. His smile was pleasant, but there was something predatory behind his eyes. She smiled and gave a slight curtsey in response, then made her way back to her father and Captain Langen.

The two had been conversing casually as they waited for the marines to conclude their search. Upon seeing her, Orin interrupted himself and introduced his daughter to the captain.

"Captain Langen, this is my daughter, Hailey."

Hailey curtsied to the captain, who smiled at her and tipped his hat.

"A lovely girl," he remarked to Orin. Hailey blushed a little, though she knew the compliment was only a formality.

A marine came up beside them.

"Sir, we found something in the captain's quarters you should see."

Hailey felt as if a vice had been applied to her neck and was starting to squeeze. She shifted uncomfortably, still feeling the weight of her guilt in her waistband.

The captain nodded to the marine, who turned and went back to the cabin. Langen's smile and rosy cheeks did not alter as he addressed Orin.

"Join us, please." Again, this was a formality. Langen was not asking so much as telling him.

Orin nodded and went to his cabin, followed by Langen and a nervous Hailey. She found herself reaching back and touching the book hidden under her shirt every few seconds, making sure that it was still there.

The sergeant stepped to the captain and saluted as they entered. The other marines stood rigidly at attention like cocked pistols. Hailey knew that in such a small space, Captain Langen need only give the word, and the marines would spring and bring the hammer down on both her and Orin without a moment's hesitation.

"Found a couple hidden compartments with contraband, sir."

The sergeant pointed to the cabinet behind the hinged portrait of Hailey's mother, and her heart began to pound. The cabinet door had been pried open with a crowbar. The books had been removed and placed on the table. Beside the stack of books stood a rather large and old-looking bottle of wine, presumably hidden in another compartment in the cabin that Hailey had not found.

Walking over to the table, Captain Langen looked over the books.

"I see. And the... item?" He looked up at the sergeant, raising an eyebrow expectantly.

"No, sir," the sergeant replied, letting his eyes drop. He stood rigidly, waiting for the next order. The seargent looked like an attack dog patiently waiting for his master to set him loose. Hailey and Orin both looked at the captain, neither of them able to hide their fear.

Captain Langen looked over the books and the wine on the table, let out a sigh that slumped his shoulders forward, and then addressed the sergeant.

"Very well, then, sergeant. Tell my first mate, Mr. Grahl to escort the *Arrow* to port. I'm going to stay on board and ask some questions. Be sure to meet me on the docks when we arrive."

He waved his hand, and the sergeant and other marines saluted and quickly marched out of the cabin, closing the door behind them.

Langen turned to Orin and smiled. They were alone.

"I hope you don't mind company on the way back to port," Langen said.

Hailey didn't know what was going on, but she didn't like it.

"No, sir," was all Orin could say.

He had been stone silent, watching the whole thing unfold with a grim face. The second he saw they had found the cabinet, he knew he was in trouble. Smuggling contra-band of any kind could land you in irons on a good day. Having contraband books usually got you hanged.

Hailey knew it all too well and stood quietly in a panic, feeling the book bite into her back as the two men ignored her.

Langen simply smiled at him. "Good. It looks as if we have some things to talk about." He slapped Orin's shoulder jovially and made his way over to the table of books.

The captain ran his fingers admiringly over the spines of the books stacked on the table as Hailey and Orin just stared at the man, terrified.

Langen pulled up the captain's chair and sat down at the table, bringing a book closer to him as though a prize. He looked up to see the two of them standing over him and motioned to the bed and the chair across the room.

"Please, sit!" They did as they were told.

Langen smiled at them as Orin pulled the chair up to the table, and Hailey sat at the end the bed. Then he began picking up the other books one by one and eyeing them, muttering their titles to himself.

"Ah, the *History of Naval Battles of the War for Independence*. I haven't read this one. I have a few others that Havasham wrote, but not this one. I simply love the detail he puts in his work."

Orin was in shock. Was he being invited to discuss forbidden books with his would-be executioner? He chuckled at the absurdity of it all.

"Glad to find someone who appreciates a good book," said Orin.

The mood had lightened considerably, and Captain Langen relaxed into the chair and made himself more comfortable. Hailey shifted on the end of the cot, trying to covertly shift the book so it sat more comfortably in her waistband.

"Thank you. Say, is that Iconen wine?" Langen picked up the bottle, eyeing it with a bit of mirth.

"It is." Orin smiled at him.

Langen gave a short laugh of delight and smiled brightly. "It's been an age since I have had some good wine and a talk about books. These days, what with all the restrictions, you just don't get that many readers anymore."

Orin nodded his agreement as Langen crossed the room to retrieve a couple of glasses he had spotted.

As Langen worked the cork, Orin thought about the wine. He had been saving it to celebrate a special occasion. He supposed, however, missing a date with a noose seemed to be good enough occasion as any.

Hailey watched it all with muted fascination. She was too young for wine, but had seen her parents and grandparents enjoy a few glasses. The bottle looked old and special. She had heard that shipbuilders often gave the new captain a bottle of wine for luck when they delivered a ship. This bit of luck seemed to be paying off.

The two men took long, appreciative sips and relaxed a bit in their chairs.

Captain Langen set down his glass and started looking through the books again. Orin looked them over as well, taking inventory. The one book he was looking for was not there. He turned and looked at Hailey, but she wouldn't meet his eye.

Langen noticed Orin's gaze, and followed it. It wasn't quite proper for a couple of sailors to be drinking and telling stories around a lady.

"Ah, yes, well, we shouldn't keep the young lady. I'm sure there are other things she would rather be doing than listening to two old men sit and talk. Why don't you be a good girl and go out with the crew on deck?"

Hailey nodded and started for the door. Her hand was almost at the door when Captain Langen called her back.

"One second, young lady."

She turned slowly, the fear and guilt flowing though her veins making it hard to move.

"The book."

She swallowed hard. He'd noticed the book hidden in her waistband. What was she going to do? He looked at her for a long moment, then smiled. He held up her primer.

"I'm sure you wouldn't want to leave without this."

He offered it to her.

She curtsied and mumbled, "Thank you."

She took the book, but he held it for a moment until she looked at him.

"Books are very important, aren't they?"

Her voice caught in her throat. She could feel both of the men's gazes on her.

She could only nod.

Captain Langen released the book with a laugh and said, "That's a good girl. Run along now."

She curtsied again and darted to the door, never so glad to be leaving her father's cabin in all of her life.

"Delightful girl." The captain chuckled.

"Thank you, sir."

"She join you often? On your sails?"

"Every chance she gets."

"And her mother?"

"Died three years ago in the incident at Cowl's Ridge."

The captain grunted and frowned. Cowl's Ridge was an incident that had left a bad taste in everyone's mouth.

"I'm sorry to hear of it."

"Thank you, sir." Orin took a sip of his wine.

There was a silence that hung in the room for a moment as the two men reflected on the incident at Cowl's Ridge. Violent protests erupted after it happened. It was a sore incident that both Crown and civilian were eager to forget. Cowl's Ridge was an old wound that every now and then reappeared and renewed its presence with a lance of pain. It was a scar on the mind of all.

Langen broke the silence.

"We received reports that the captain of the *Arrow* had come into possession of a certain item we are looking for. You wouldn't happen to know what it is, would you?"

Orin gave him his best puzzled look.

"No, sir."

Langen's face had changed again from rosy and jovial to dark and tense.

"And you have no other hidden compartments that we haven't found?"

"No, sir."

Just as quickly as the storm came to Langen's face, it passed, and he resumed his rosy smile. He reached across the table and refilled Orin's glass.

"Well, good! Now, let's drink, and we can talk about how you came upon these books."

HAILEY STEPPED BACK into the sunlight and could see that the *Vigilant* had just moved off from them. Both the *Arrow* crew and the *Vigilant's* decks were abuzz with motion as they raised sails for the port of Daden.

On the stern of the *Vigilant* she noticed the tall, dapper man looking back at their ship. He tipped his hat at her again, but this time turned and walked away before she could curtsey a reply. It occurred to Hailey that it was as if he was simply saying goodbye for now.

Hailey's thoughts returned to the man in her father's cabin. The Crown was looking for the book, that much was certain. Langen had asked if they had found the item. What else could it be but the book? Crown ships often stopped ships coming into ports, but more often than not, they were looking for a bribe to look the other way on trumped-up infractions. This was different. This was a hunt.

Her dad did not like dealing with the Queen's officers, but as head of a merchant guild, he spoke with them on a daily basis when back in port. Langen was different. His smile didn't go all the way to his eyes, and that made her not trust him. He may not have left any marines on the ship with them, but Hailey was certain they were watching, and if anything was amiss, the *Vigilant* would be on top of them at a moment's notice.

Why had he stayed behind? The portly Captain Langen didn't strike her as the physical type; he was the kind of man who knew that words could be deadlier than his sword. Hailey suspected that he knew full well that Orin at one time had the book and opted to stay to sniff it out. She suspected the captain would question Orin about it after several drinks loosened his tongue. Thankfully, her mountain of a father could handle not only his wine better than most in their village, but he could also more than handle any book-loving sea captain who asked too many questions.

The book!

Instinctively, Hailey reached to make sure the book didn't show too much in the lines of her shirt. She felt for it as discreetly as she could, looking as though she were trying to smooth out her shirt but looking awkward while doing it.

She was thankful the crew was too occupied with their duties and getting under way to pay any attention to her. The book was still there, its soft leather and cold silver resting against her back.

Was this book a piece of the Queen's magic? She had seen many Crown representatives perform miracles during her travels with her father. Their officials and nobles could project their images across whole other continents to talk with one another with magic mirrors. They could summon light from globes with a wave of their hand. They rode around towns in coaches that had horses of steel that never tired or hungered. They seemed to never get sick or age.

A book that wrote itself and projected living maps seemed to pale in comparison. Why would the Crown dispatch warships to search vessels for something so minor?

The ghost pirates were searching for the book, too, if she were to believe what the book told her. They were coming for it. They were coming for her.

But what about this book made it such a great prize? Why would the Queen come down from her high tower to search for it? Why would the dead rise from their graves to find it?

# CHAPTER 4

s the *Arrow* neared the dock, Hailey knew she was in trouble. She wasn't afraid of the marines who waited for them on the docks in their bright red uniforms as the ship slid into its slip. She wasn't worried about her father grabbing her the moment Captain Langen left the ship. She was, however, worried about the scowling face that looked for her from the docks. Grandmother Rose was not happy.

The moment the gangway hit the dock, Grandmother Rose shoved her way past the marines without a glance and stormed onto the deck of the ship. Her eyes were instantly on Hailey, and the look of distaste worsened.

"Child, who let you out of the cabin looking like that?" Before Hailey could respond, she continued, "No matter, dear. Where is your father?"

She didn't wait for a response. Instead she barged her way to the captain's quarters, where Captain Langen and Orin were just beginning to emerge from the doorway like a pair of old friends. She moved in on her son like a hawk, Hailey firmly in tow.

"Orin! You are late!"

It took a moment for Orin to focus on her, but when he did, he sobered immediately under her scornful gaze.

"You said come as quickly as I could, and I did," Orin mumbled, trying to conceal his slight slur. His mother was one of the most prim and proper women the western world had ever known, but it never stopped her from getting what she wanted. Her wit and sharp tongue were legendary. Her will was iron-bound, and she was without mercy when opposed. After a lifetime of tongue lashing, even the mighty oak that was Orin fell to her scorn and withered then fell under her gaze.

Hailey had grown to resent Grandmother Rose for it, especially now that Rose was standing there glaring at her. Hailey knew her grandmother meant well, but Grandmother Rose's methods were merciless at best and cruel at their worst, and it had taken a toll on both Hailey and her father since she'd moved in. Hailey watched the once confident and bold man that was her father slowly being chipped away, crumbling under the relentless pecking and harping of Grandmother Rose.

Sensing the tension, Captain Langen stepped forward and came to his fellow captain's aid by taking Rose's hand.

"Madam, I believe I am at fault. I had to detain him for questioning. Queen's business, ma'am. Please forgive me." He then removed his hat and bowed his head low, having placed his forehead on her hand.

Grandmother Rose burst into full bloom. Her features softened with a smile, and her cheeks glowed with happiness. It was not often that someone from the Crown, let alone someone with as high a status as a Crown ship's captain, would bow and beg forgiveness of anyone less than a noble. Grandmother Rose was a firm believer in decorum and knew her place. She recognized just what a great honor this was and was truly touched.

"My dear sir, you honor me." She curtsied.

Captain Langen stood up and put his hat back on. "The honor was all mine, my lady." He smiled at her, but Hailey noted that again, the smile didn't quite reach his eyes.

During the exchange, the marines had come aboard once more and stood at attention behind Rose; her yellow dress seemed to glow in contrast to the red of the Royal Marines.

Langen addressed both Orin and Rose. "I'm afraid I must take my leave of you. Matters to tend to, you know."

Rose beamed at him. "I understand."

Captain Langen addressed the sergeant. "Be sure to collect all the books and bring them aboard my ship." He gave Orin a sly smile and wink. "The wine didn't make it, I'm afraid."

With a nod from the sergeant, one of the marines moved quickly into the captain's quarters and returned with the small stack of books. Orin and Hailey's treasured volumes of history were becoming history before their very eyes. Orin and Hailey watched helplessly as their treasured leather-bound volumes were cradled by the marines and carried out of the cabin.

Orin looked ill and started to sputter. Given his station as the head of one of the largest merchant guilds in the west, he could have protested. Surely allowances could be made, he thought. Orin looked pleadingly at the man whom he had come to think of as a friend as well as fellow book aficionado but was rebuffed.

The cold, hard look that Langen gave him in return and the grave stillness in which he delivered it amounted to an altogether wordless reply. Orin knew that if he opened his mouth, even his status and social standing would not save him from the hangman's noose that day.

"I'm sure you understand. Queen's business and all," Langen said, nodding slowly. The eyes of the marines searched them both, like dogs trained to sense if anything was amiss, ready to loose themselves of their burdens and jump into action. Orin, stupefied and defeated, bobbed his head like a puppet, matching Langen's movement.

Both Hailey and Orin watched as the collection of banned books, stack by stack, were carried out and down the gangway and out of their lives. It had taken Orin and his wife a lifetime to collect them. Orin looked and felt as though he had just lost a child.

Seeing this, Langen patted Orin on the shoulder and leaned in, whispering in confidence to him, "Not to worry! I'm sure our paths will cross again soon. You are welcome to come visit them at any time."

He stepped back, bowed to the three of them, tipped his cap, and waddled down the gangway, following the marines back to his ship to look over his new prizes.

Hailey reached back reflexively and felt for the book, checking to see that it was still in place. Hailey wondered if it were only the books that would have been marched down the gangway if the Marines had found it.

"Hailey!" her grandmother snapped, bringing both her and Orin out of their daze. Hailey jumped with a start, hoping that her grandmother had not noticed her feeling for the book. Even if she had, she dismissed it quickly and grabbed Hailey's hand.

"Come along, we have to have you fitted for your dress for the party tomorrow night.

"Party?" Orin asked, folding his arms.

"Yes! We are hosting a party to greet the new bishop in the colonial mansion. That is why I asked you to come back so quickly. I've been up to my neck in preparations trying to get it all ready."

Orin opened his mouth to speak, but Rose cut him off.

"No sense talking about it. Right now I need to get Hailey

to the dressmaker to get a dress made." She patted Orin on the cheek, turned from him, and snapped at Hailey, "Well? Get your things!"

Hailey knew better than to delay when her grandmother was in a hurry. She shot past the two of them, went into the hold, and quickly reappeared with her duffel bag.

"Now wait a minute. I need to talk with Hailey," Orin said as he tried to stand between Grandmother Rose and Hailey, but Rose evaded him quickly.

Though Hailey's grandmother was a little old lady, her grip was of iron, and her will was just as unbendable. She grabbed Hailey's arm and pulled her along, around Orin, and down to the gangplank.

"You can talk with her later, we need to go. Now. Come, girl," Rose called over her shoulder.

And with that, Orin lost his second child of the day, this one to his mother. As with his books, he could only stand on the deck and watch his mother take his child in tow and raced down the docks and into the crowds of the city.

The town of Daden was one of the first colonies on the isle of Arwend, so its city center was larger, greener, and more established than other colonies. It had been built into a prosperous center for commerce and trade. Being one of the first stops out from the capital city of Davos on the other side of the globe, it became the hub for the growth and expansion of the "new lands" found to the west of Phesin.

The city center was surrounded by a giant canopy of green leaves, which had formed over the years as the tree homes planted by the early settlers bloomed and flourished with the help of shapers like Grandmother Rose. With knowledge passed down from the Ancients, shapers manipulated the quickly growing trees into the large homes, hotels, and businesses that made up Daden. The shapers coexisted with their environment instead of conquering it, just as the

Ancients had wanted. It took iron-willed people like Hailey's grandmother to help mold it into the lush green haven it was.

The shaded roadways winding up from the docks were clogged full of horse-drawn carriages and carts carrying cargo from the ships to be sold in the market. The additional crush of passengers from the various vessels pressing their way into the town only led to even more congestion.

Hailey's grandmother might have been a practitioner of charm and decorum and a bastion of the social order, but not when she was in a hurry. She yanked Hailey through the crowds, weaving her way up the long ramp to the town square.

Once in the square, Rose slackened her pace, but not her grip on Hailey, as they plunged into the heart of the market square. Grandmother Rose and Hailey plowed onward, determined to make headway against the tide of people who were ahead of them in the section that was known to locals as Farmer's Row. Hailey was bombarded by the sights, sounds, and smells of the marketplace, telling her senses and her heart that she was home.

Spices and fruits from all around the world were spread in a colorful array in bins, filling the air with a bright and spicy perfume. Hopeful sellers chattered with reluctant buyers as they dickered over prices of their wares. Meat vendors called out, trying to tempt customers into buying fresh cuts from their butcher stalls.

The crowd flowed forward, the current of people carrying them along slowly through Farmer's Row. Each stall became an eddy into which a few people would drift off as the human river ran its course. Grandmother Rose made sure to keep an iron grip on her granddaughter as she plunged them through the heart of the stream of life, determined to get to the dressmaker.

# CHAPTER 5

*H*ailey didn't play with dress-up dolls growing up. She liked being a dress-up doll for her grandmother even less. She stood on a small platform in front of the mirrors in the dress shop, while Anton, an impish, gray-haired, and bespectacled tailor, danced about her, taking her measurements and pinning fabric. In the mirrors, she could see her grandmother pacing about in worry.

"Oh, Anton, do you think it will be ready in time?"

The little man mumbled consonants around a mouth full of pins, sounding neither positive nor negative.

"It simply must be done in time. Everyone is going to be there. It will be the event of the season."

"Ow!" Hailey yelped at accidentally being stuck with a pin.

"Stn stll," was all the little man mumbled, grabbing for another pin out of his mouth.

Hailey couldn't decide whom to glare at first, him or her grandmother. Both seemed equally guilty at that time, so she settled on glaring at everyone, including herself, in the mirror.

She hated herself for not defending herself against her grandmother's constant bullying. Grandmother Rose was trying to make her into something she wasn't, but she didn't have the courage to say no.

She knew the moment she did, her grandmother would just redouble her efforts and eventually break her will. Rose was like the sea constantly pounding on the shore—eventually, even the toughest stone would crumble.

"Hailey, I've set it up so that most of the eligible bachelors are going to be there early that evening, which will give you ample time to speak with them. Choosing a future husband is a difficult task and takes time. This will give you a good opportunity to get to know your potential suitors and help you decide when the time comes."

Hailey knew that her grandmother meant well and was doing this out of love, but she really didn't want to think about marriage right now, if ever. She had never really taken an interest in boys.

Grandmother Rose was just following the doctrine that the Church of the Ancestors, the only church and educator in the world, drilled into their minds for ages. It was said it was written in the Book of the Ancestors that true happiness can only be achieved through elevating one's status in life. Since women couldn't hold any position of real meaning, marrying the right man was the only way to advance themselves.

The book was said to be a wondrous thing handed down to them from the Ancients. It was a magical book that contained vast amounts of knowledge that only the Church and the Queen could read. It was a book very similar to the one Hailey still hid beneath her clothes in the changing room.

"I don't see why I can't just be a captain like my dad."

Anton stopped working on the dress and looked at her

disapprovingly. Hailey looked at them both, embarrassed. Hailey's grandmother broke the long silence.

"Heavens, no, child. Have you lost your sense? Whoever heard of a woman captain?"

Grandmother Rose looked embarrassed for her, and Anton went back to work on the dress.

"So you met Grandfather at one of these gala balls?" Hailey knew the answer; she just felt like lashing back a little. But Grandmother Rose didn't seem to notice.

"Stars above, no. If I had had the opportunities you have, I might be in the governor's mansion!" she tittered to herself. The little man continued to circle Hailey as she stood as till as she could. "No, I met your grandfather at one of the smaller merchant events. He was the best pick there, the son of a strong merchant family on the rise. I was nothing more than the daughter of a farmer—and he had to borrow the dress I wore that evening. Your grandfather was surrounded by women, each one plainer than the next and trying to get his attention. None of us were very highly ranked in society, and he and his family were a step up. Quite the catch."

She trailed off and stared for a moment, forgetting herself and becoming lost in the memory. Hailey stood watching her reflection in the mirror. Catching herself, Grandmother Rose shook her head and continued.

"Well, I worked my way through the swarm of ladies and made him accidentally spill his punch on me. Of course, being a gentleman, he went with me to the kitchen to get a towel and some water to clean up my borrowed dress. Once we were alone, I was able to charm him enough that he sought me out the next day after the party. We began our courtship, and a few months later, we were married." She sighed. "Best move I ever made," she said, looking wistful.

"So you only went after Grandfather for his position?"

"Well, he was handsome, too, dear. But yes."

"What about love?"

"Don't be silly, dear, be practical. In life, you shouldn't let your heart steer when the head is needed. Marry for position, reliability, and the ability to provide for your family. If you have all that and an open ear to your suggestions, then naturally love will follow. My dear, his hand may steer the ship, but you are the one who sets the course."

"What about Dad and Mom?"

Her grandmother's face fell into a frown. "Yes, well, that was your father's mistake...." She caught herself and decided to plow on. "We were doing quite well; I had even set up for him to meet with a noble's young daughter, but he had a mind of his own. Met your mother in some tavern over in Jakar, the daughter of some boat maker." She shook her head. "Completely ruined my plans."

Hailey was about to reply, but was cut off. The little man took the pins out of his mouth and declared, "All done!" He helped Hailey down from the platform and scooted her towards the changing closet. "Go and change out of that if you could. And be careful!"

Once inside the changing closet, Hailey could hear her grandmother harassing the little man.

"Oh dear, Anton, do you think you can have the dress ready in time?"

"I will do my very best, madam. There are several other dresses ahead of it because of the ball, but I should get to it in time."

"I see." The two moved away from the mirrors and towards the front of the store.

Hailey opened the door of the closet just in time to see her grandmother lean closer to Anton.

"Maybe this will help with our place in line." She held out a small bag, heavy with coins.

The small man smiled and nodded his head a bit. He put the bag of coins in his pocket without even looking at them. Anton then took her by her hands and looked up at her as he patted them.

"I think it will help nicely."

# CHAPTER 6

Hailey and Grandmother Rose came out of the dressmaker's house and entered a plaza surrounded by food carts of every size. The plaza was littered with tables and chairs for people to stop and eat. Hailey knew just which cart they were going to. Her grandmother always held to the tradition of having a good, stiff cup of tea before she began the day's shopping. Hailey wondered if she went there more for the gossip with the ladies around the cart rather than the tea itself; Rose could gossip for hours.

They approached the teacart, which was already encircled with several other older ladies, many of whom her grandmother knew well. Several ladies called and waved to Rose as they approached. Rose stopped just short of the group, greeted them, and proudly introduced them all to her granddaughter. All of the ladies had met Hailey several times over the course of the years, but whether it was due to decorum, formality, or failing memories, the introductions were made all the same. Many of the ladies had known Hailey since she was little, but they still greeted her as if it were the first time.

Hailey vaguely remembered a rather dry section of her mother's primer that talked about the formalities of greetings and the benefits of encouraging such behavior. To Hailey it made the ladies seem dim and flighty at best and thoughtless at worst.

Then came the embarrassing questions, most of them about either courting young men or the fact that she was no longer a little girl anymore. They pointed out Hailey's height and curves, despite her wearing baggy clothes to hide them. They remarked on her long legs and her beautiful mane of hair, which they thought it a shame for her to keep hidden in a braid most of the time. She felt as though she were one of the sides of beef in the market she'd just passed, with each lady shouting out her best and worst cuts.

Mercifully, the conversation changed to her grandmother's party, and Rose loosened her grip on Hailey, allowing her to slip away from the group. She made her way to one of the more secluded tables in the square, out of sight of the ladies at the teacart. After that embarrassing exchange, she wanted to hide, or if anything, blend into the crowd for a bit.

She looked around to be sure no one had noticed her too much. People around her and across the way didn't even bother to look in her direction. Most people were too busy with their own lives and in their own heads to stop and notice someone sitting alone at a table. In the great throng of humanity that rushed about her, she was all but invisible to them. Her grandmother and the ladies were still talking up a storm and would be at it for a while. Hailey immediately thought to look at the book again. She pulled it out from her waistband and placed it on the table, confident that no one would notice. The latches popped open and she opened the book, and once again she was greeted with blank pages.

She looked up, ready to slap shut the book if the living map that she had seen before appeared again. Looking around, she slowly opened it and there was no map. Hailey sighed with relief. She didn't want anything weird happening in public, but her curiosity about the book was overwhelming.

The book was still blank and unchanged. She found herself wondering if she had imagined the whole thing when words began to bubble up on the page.

*YOU DIDN'T IMAGINE IT. I AM TALKING TO YOU.*

Reading the words, she thought she heard a little voice in her head saying them. It was a voice she had not heard before. Hailey tilted her head and looked quizzically at the book. She didn't think she'd said anything out loud.

*YOU DIDN'T SAY ANYTHING OUT LOUD*

Could this book hear her thoughts?

*OF COURSE I CAN HEAR YOUR THOUGHTS.*
*I TOLD YOU:*
*YOU ARE THE NAVIGATOR.*

Hailey now focused her thoughts at the book. She found herself squinting at it, feeling as though she had to beam her thoughts to it, that there was some trick to will it to hear her.

*NO NEED TO SQUINT OR STRAIN. I CAN HEAR YOU*
*PERFECTLY WELL. RELAX YOUR FACE. YOU'LL DRAW*
*ATTENTION. YOU DON'T WANT ANYONE TO NOTICE*
*YOU, DO YOU?*

Hailey stopped and looked around, letting the features on her face relax.

*MUCH BETTER*

Hailey thought to it, *Who are you?*

*I AM THE NAVIGATOR'S BOOK, OF COURSE. I HOLD THE RECORDS AND PERSONAL WRITINGS FOR THE GREAT RACHEL FERON.*

*Who is that?*

*OH. WELL MAYBE YOU KNOW HER AS RACHEL OF THE RED SASH?*

The book must have registered that Hailey did not know the name.

*NO?*
*SIGH*
*MAYBE YOU KNOW HER BY HER TITLE, THEN. SHE WAS KNOWN AS THE PIRATE QUEEN.*

Upon the reading the last three words, she felt her skin grow cold and pale. *That's why the pirates are coming for the book!* she thought.

*YES.*
*AND YOU, OF COURSE.*
*THEY ARE COMING FOR YOU AS WELL.*
*AS THE ONLY ONE WHO CAN OPEN AND USE ME, OF COURSE THEY WOULD HAVE TO COME FOR YOU.*
*YOU ARE THE NAVIGATOR, AFTER ALL.*

*Why do you keep calling me the Navigator? My name is Hailey.*

### BECAUSE THAT IS WHO YOU ARE.
### ONLY A NAVIGATOR CAN OPEN AND OPERATE ME, HAILEY.

*Why me?*

### BECAUSE YOU ARE SPECIAL

Hailey never thought of herself as special.

### YOU'VE ALWAYS BEEN A GOOD NAVIGATOR, RIGHT? A NATURAL. ALMOST AS IF IT WAS IN YOUR BLOOD.

Hailey found herself nodding and remembering all the times her father had praised her skills with the map and compass.

### TAKE A LOOK AT THIS

Above the book, a smaller version of the living map appeared. Hailey looked around in a panic, afraid someone would see. She was just about to slam the book shut when she saw the page flashing and words displaying:

### RELAX!
### ONLY YOU CAN SEE THE MAP, SILLY GIRL.

Hailey looked back to the image. Again she saw the map of the world floating in the air before her. It seemed alive and crawling with information. The map was dotted with ships out at sea, trade winds, water temperatures, and cloud patterns, which all swirled and danced before her.

If she focused her attention on one thing, the map zoomed in on the object. She focused on a ship out at sea, crossing from the capital city of Davos, heading to the northwest. The image zoomed in to an image of the boat; its odd conical sails were darker than she expected. The information beside it read *"The Virtuous."* Under that, it showed that the boat was headed to the port of McKinnett in Aibronne. The calculated time for the journey was just over five weeks. Following the path of their course, Hailey could see that they were headed on a longer, inefficient route, tacking on additional and unnecessary time to its journey. She wondered if that was intentional or due to navigator error.

She looked away from the ship, and the image snapped back to the view of the whole world. The sudden change almost gave her vertigo. She looked back to the book to see words awaiting her.

> ***MORE THAN LIKELY YOU ARE RIGHT IN THINKING IT TO BE A NAVIGATIONAL ERROR, I'M AFRAID. IT LOOKS AS IF THEIR MORNING READINGS WERE OFF A DEGREE OR TWO.***

She smiled. That's why she'd been up in the mast that morning, checking and rechecking her figures. It always kept them true to course. It seemed that the captain was either not an early riser or just careless.

*I thought you said you were a journal. All I see is this map.*

> ***YOU HAVEN'T ASKED ME FOR ANYTHING ELSE***

*Well, what else is there?*

### *YOU COULD READ RACHEL'S DIARY AND NOTES.*

*Why would I want to read that?*

### *WELL, WHAT GOOD IS A MAP WHEN YOU HAVE NO DESTINATION?*

Hailey puzzled over this for a bit. What would be the destination? She mulled it over, but the book gave no reaction. Her mind raced about the very few things that the book had told her about Rachel. She was a female sea captain, something Hailey had never heard of before except in her own fantasies. She was also a pirate. Not just any pirate, she was a queen. If she was anything like the the Veiled Queen in Davos, she had tons of magical items and hordes of treasures. Did that mean there are directions to a treasure here?

She glanced at the page and got her answer.

### *YES. FAR LARGER AND MORE IMPORTANT THAT YOU CAN IMAGINE, MY DEAR.*

Hailey's eyes went wide. No wonder everyone was looking for this book! She wanted to ask more questions, but the pages cleared and displayed a simple and blunt warning.

### *HIDE ME! YOU ARE BEING WATCHED!*

She snapped the book shut and quickly looked about her, then she felt the smiling eyes upon her. Across the pavilion, on the other side of the river of people, sat the dapper gentleman in the velvety blue-and-gold suit she had seen on the deck of the *Vigilant*, watching her and drinking his tea. Slowly. Deliberately. Hailey froze. The man blinked, smiled his shark-like smile at her, tipped his hat to her once again, got up, and left.

Hailey could feel her pulse in her ears. Who *was* that man? Had he followed her, or was it a coincidence? She didn't want to stick around to find out. She quickly stood and shoved the book under her shirt. She had just turned back in the direction of her grandmother, when she froze in the gaze of another pair of eyes watching her.

In the doorway of a store stood a tall, muscular young man close to her age leaning against the frame and looking right at her, arms folded. His face betrayed no emotion, just observation. Hailey thought him to be beautiful, but that beauty seemed to have a flaw. There was something not right about him. She kept her gaze locked on him, trying to figure it out. After a couple of seconds, she noticed that the boy's eyes were a light almond color. Too light for normal eyes. They looked unnatural, almost ghostly.

As he stood there, arms crossed, she could see a glint of metal that caught her eye on the ring finger of his left hand. It was a ring with the same silver and ruby skull design that was on the book's cover. He stood perfectly still, staring at her as if he wanted to see what she would do.

Hailey broke her gaze with him the second a hand clamped around her arm. She jumped and screamed, but the hand did not let go.

"Hailey! What's gotten into you? That is not how we behave in public! I've been looking all over for you. Come on! We have a few more stores we need to get to before sundown."

Grandmother Rose quickly turned and plunged back into the river of the crowd, pulling the shaken Hailey along with her. She only had the briefest of moments to look over her shoulder before being swallowed by the mass of people.

The boy was gone, his eyes still haunting her.

# CHAPTER 7

The sun was low in the sky when Hailey and her grandmother finished at the market and began making their way up the winding road to their family home. As the last rays of light touched the leaves of their house, Hailey noticed that in her absence her home had grown slightly in the months she had been gone.

The tree they had shaped over time into their home was already large and wide, but now the branches looked to be a little taller overhead. This homestead was once planted and trained by the first colonists, so it was one of the larger homes in the area. All of the tree homes grew very quickly when tended to by professional shapers like her grandmother, but they wouldn't grow indefinitely. In time the tree would stop growing and fossilize, turning into stone as the shapers designed it.

Thinking on this, Hailey felt the irony that her grandmother was trying to do the same thing to her as she did to the tree homes. She would shape them until they no longer changed.

Sitting in the shade of the tree home, muttering to himself and struggling with a tangle of knotted ropes, was Hailey's father.

Hailey was thankful that her father hadn't inherited his disposition from his mother. Had her father turned out like Grandmother Rose, Hailey would have run away from home a long time ago.

She had been avoiding her father long enough. She knew she would have to talk to him sometime. In fact, she wanted to talk to him, to tell him what the book said, yet still she hesitated. A little part in her was afraid that he would be mad at her. That he'd dismiss her and wouldn't want to listen. She had to talk to him, however, and she may as well do it when he was in a good mood.

Hailey broke away from her grandmother and joined her father on the bench. Grandmother Rose was too preoccupied with all the thoughts of things that needed doing before the party to even notice Hailey's absence anyway. He continued to struggle with the ropes, all the time watching Grandmother Rose pass into the house.

Orin leaned over and murmured to Hailey, "She looks as if she's in one of her moods. I think it might be a good time for us to go for a walk on the beach." He set down the ball of ropes and got up.

"But Grandmother Rose told me on the way home not to go anywhere," Hailey said.

He looked up at her for a moment. "Is that so? Well, on the boat I told you we needed to talk. My order was first." He winked at her.

They both knew that if they stuck around, Grandmother Rose would find something for them to do, so they quickly made their way around to the backyard, past the kitchen house and to the well-worn path that led down to the ocean.

Halfway down the path they could hear faint calls for them going unanswered.

They quietly walked side by side along the shore as the sun began to set, the only sounds between them the frothing sound of the waves crashing on the shore and the sand squeaking beneath their feet.

After the sun went down, he would occasionally stop and point out stars and constellations. Orin recounted stories about each of them and how they traced the path in the sky to where their ancestors once fell to this world. Hailey had heard these stories before, both from him and also at the church. She didn't tell him or correct him when he missed a few things, just silently listened as though it were the first time.

The story of the original Ancestors was a tragic one that ended with a fall from great heights from which they could never re-ascend. All their descendants could do afterward was look up at the heavens they were once a part of. The hope was that the Ancestors would smile down on their achievements and, after they died, raise descendants up into the heavens as new stars in the night sky. Hailey wondered where her mother's was and where her father's star would be after he was gone. They both fell into silence.

There was one constellation in particular in his story her father would always neglect to mention, though it was fairly prominent and low in the sky. It was the one with two red stars that looked as though they were eyes looking down on them. It was the group that sailors used to navigate the northern waters --the constellation they called Ghost Pirate.

Hailey's father broke the silence as they walked. "You know my dad used to take me for walks like this when I was younger. We would walk the shore for hours, without saying a word."

Hailey looked over at her father as they walked. He just looked up at the sky, then continued, "I think it was because he was giving me room to talk. I always appreciated that. Growing up with your grandmother, always asking questions and demanding things, it was a nice change. It made me feel more grown up."

He fell into silence once more. Hailey studied the sand as they walked. Her father patiently walked by her side. She knew that he wanted her to tell him about taking the book. She wanted to tell him, but she was still afraid. She wanted to pretend for just a little bit longer that it wasn't real, but the book's words flashed in her mind.

*THIS IS REAL. THEY ARE COMING.*

Orin looked down at her and, trying a different tack, started a different conversation.

"Did I ever tell you about how your mother and I met?"

He had, but Hailey always loved to hear it, so she shook her head as he sighed and fell back into memory.

"It was because of a book, actually."

Hailey's head whipped up and around to look at him. He had never told her that before, and the statement caught her off guard. He looked back at her and chuckled. "Don't be so surprised. You remember how much of an avid reader your mother was. I figure you're old enough to know about it now."

Hailey felt a twinge of excitement as he began to tell the story.

He'd been in Jakar looking for a boat. His father had sent him there because the boat crafters were said to be legendary. It was to be his first ship, and Grandfather Angus wanted to be sure that Orin had the best. He put him in touch with one of the oldest boat-building families there and sent him to negotiate a deal.

Arriving at port, Orin found that there was only one room available at an inn all the way on the other side of the city because there was some boat race that the nobles were staging.

He didn't know the town very well, and he only had just enough money to get the boat and pay for his room at the inn, so he spent a lot of time in the tavern reading. It just so happened that a beautiful woman with raven black hair worked there. She saw him reading and told him about her love for books.

Orin stayed there for several months as his boat was being built, and he and the girl from the tavern grew closer. They had a lot in common. A love of reading, collecting banned books, humor—she was wonderful. She was every-thing he had ever dreamed of in a woman.

It was only after the boat was finished that he found out that she was the builder's daughter. It turned out that she knew why Orin was there and asked her dad to take his time building Orin's ship so they could get to know one another better.

"It worked," Orin said, "because by the time her father was finished, I had asked her to marry me."

Orin grinned to himself, warm in the memory of it.

"And?" asked Hailey.

"After her father christened the boat, I thought of staying and setting up shop there, but something happened."

Hailey kept looking forward, avoiding his gaze.

"She came to me one night, all in a panic, and said we had to leave Jakar right away. I couldn't understand what would scare her so much and make her want to abandon her friends and family like that, but I was in love and didn't want to question it. She told me that there was a book that we had to hide, that someone was coming for it, and for her. I don't think I had ever seen your mother so afraid. We sailed out that night with a small crew whom we gathered in the tavern and sailed here, never looking back."

They walked on in silence, the shushing sound of the moving sand beneath their feet and the moist smell of seaweed and salt in the air. One question rolled over and over in her head like the surf churning off the shore.

"So what happened to the book?" Hailey finally asked.

Orin gave a slight grin. "That creepy thing? Well, at first we sent it away for a friend to hold on to. Your mother thought it important that she not be around it for some reason. That friend ended up trading it with someone else, and we lost touch with it. Until recently."

Her father cleared his throat, then continued. "My old friend and sailing partner, Seamus Pike, stumbled on it on a trip to Aibronne. He wrote me about it, and we decided to meet up in Baron's Bay. Your mother had asked me not too long before she died to get it to you if I ever found it. I don't know what's in it or why she sent it away, but it was important enough to her that you have it, so I got it for you."

He stopped walking, and Hailey stopped beside him. With a sigh, he looked at her and said, "It's a shame it disappeared." He shrugged his shoulders and walked on, leaving Hailey standing alone for a moment.

Hailey thought he obviously knew, but wasn't saying anything. True to his word, he didn't press her like Grandmother Rose. He was giving her space to talk after he presented the facts. Hailey felt a little relieved that her dad sounded as if he was going to let the topic rest, especially since he had been planning on giving her the book anyway.

Hailey caught up with him, and they walked on in silence. Off the shore, a mist began to build just under the two red stars that made up the Skull. Hailey suddenly felt a chill and decided to ask what he knew.

"Dad, what do you know about pirates?"

She found herself staring over her shoulder at the two glowing eyes in the sky, almost as if the eyes were following her. Watching her. She shifted and felt the book still hidden in her waistband.

With every sailor, there were three things you never talked about: the Queen in the east, the storms to the west, or the ghosts of pirates waiting in the middle. They believed that the more you talked about something, the more you summoned them to you. Hailey wondered how right that was.

She looked at him apologetically as Orin stopped and gave the question quiet consideration. He turned and looked out over the ocean, its soft waves rolling in the moonlight. A slight breeze stirred his long gray ponytail as his eyes searched the water. He seemed to notice the mists gathering just off the shore.

"People say that they are just a myth. Some kind of Boogiemen created to scare children into behaving. When the King was alive, he would send out search parties for them all the time, but they never found anything. I never believed in them too much, though like any good sailor I try to avoid sailing in the mists if I can help it."

Hailey thought about the warnings she had heard as a child:

*Eyes of red*
   *of the pirate dead*
   *Are on the hunt for you.*
   *Beware the mists,*
   *And take no risks,*
   *Lest you become a ghost pirate, too.*

"I USED to hear a lot of stories about the ghost pirates from my father and other sailors in port back then. Occasionally someone would tell tale of a black ship that could be seen in the mists for a moment and then gone the next. My father's first mate swore he saw an ominous shadow of a ship on the water with no ship there. He was known to tell a tall tale or two over a few drinks in the tavern, though. They all did." He shook his head. "I never took much stock in it."

"Why not?" Hailey asked.

"Well, you see, not many who actually saw the ghost pirates lived to tell the tale. There are a few people here and there who sound more convincing than the others, but not many. Your grandfather believed in them. Said he actually ran into them. He used to talk about it to anyone who would listen. I never gave it much attention until he disappeared not long after you were born."

Hailey's eyes went wide. She could feel the cold metal of the book pressing against her back. The more her father talked, the more it seemed to get colder and bite into her skin.

He turned from her and looked at the moon reflecting on the waves and noticed that the mist off the coast was larger and getting closer still.

"He would tell us that when he was younger, there were many steamy nights like this, where the mists creep out of the cool water and dance with the warm night air. Everything off the shorelines would be covered in a thick gray blanket that ships would completely disappear into. They'd be found days later, lifeless and stripped of everything."

Hailey gasped. "What happened?"

"At first the King and noblemen thought it was some local townsfolk privateering, but there was no way. Trade was too good, and nobody was fool enough to risk sending their entire families, children and all, to the gallows for piracy.

Nobody was that stupid. Dad and the rest of the people in town thought it was the ghosts exacting revenge for what the Crown had done to them."

According to her father's history books and what she'd learned in school, Hailey knew that two hundred years ago, the King had hunted down every known pirate family. No man, woman, or child was spared the Crown's wrath. Even helping one of the suspected pirates was a death sentence. It was a lesson that the schools were quick to burn into the hearts and minds of its citizens. Piracy was a death sentence for you and your entire bloodline.

"More cargo ships kept disappearing," Orin went on, "so the Crown sent more ships to patrol the waters. The more patrols they sent, the more cargo ships would dissapear into the mists without a trace. Your grandfather reckoned that it couldn't be anyone attacking them. There was no way any mortal ship could avoid one of the patrols. A boat would have to appear out of thin air."

Orin paused, as if not sure whether to continue. "Your grandfather was on one of those ships that disappeared."

Hailey gasped.

"Actually, the way he tells it, the pirates sank it. He was just a cabin boy on a ship with a family friend, Captain Stevens. They were off the northern coast of Arwend making the run to McKinnett, when the wind died down and the mists rolled in and covered them completely. He'd traveled through mists and all kinds of weather before, but nothing like this. The fog was thick and looked like tentacles wrapping themselves around the ship. It clung to everything it touched and was cold and wet. Oddly, he said it left a taste in your mouth like sour grapes."

"And then what happened?" Hailey asked.

"Once in the mists, their compasses and navigation equipment quit working. They were trying to get their bearings, when all of a sudden there was the roar of cannons and an explosion of wood and metal on their port side. Their masts cracked and toppled to the sea. The whole crew was dazed and riddled with splinters from the shots. Then it got quiet again."

Hailey stared out at the water, seeing the mists starting to reach the rocks just off the shore, making them look like teeth popping up out of the mists. He continued.

"Then the black ship appeared. He said it looked as if it flew out of the mist silently, like an owl, and slammed into their starboard side. Your grandfather was beside the rail when it hit and was flung overboard. Fortunately he had enough wits about him to find a chunk of the mast floating in the water to hold on to and keep from drowning.

"He watched from the water as the dark figures with glowing eyes poured from the black ship onto the deck. He heard only a few cries from the crew, then it was quiet again. The ship began to smoke and burn. On the quarterdeck he saw Captain Stevens standing and shaking with his hands up in surrender. A dark figure stood and asked him something that your grandfather couldn't hear. He swore by the looks of it they were searching for something."

Hailey flinched and went wide eyed. *This is real. They are coming.*

Orin stopped and turned to her.

"Are you all right?" He shuffled back towards her.

The blood had left Hailey's face and she felt light-headed, but she waved him off. "Yeah, just…" She hugged herself and shifted uncomfortably as the book dug into her back. "Just scary, that's all."

He nodded.

"Well, poor Captain Stevens pleaded with the figure, but it did no good. It said not a word as it ran Captain Stevens through with its sword. The sight of it made your grandfather scream."

She shivered despite the warm night.

"That's when the thing turned its hateful, glowing red eyes on him. It leaned over the rail and looked at your grandfather floating helplessly in the water. When telling the tale, he would go into eerie detail about every moment of that event. It used to scare me. He would talk about the creature's glowing skull for a face or its ragged and torn dark clothes or the terrible black cutlass it held in its hands. He even talked about little things, like the rings it had on its bony fingers."

"Rings?" Hailey asked.

Orin looked at her for a moment, puzzled, and Hailey ducked her head a bit. She was slightly embarrassed asking him, but she had to know. "What did they look like?"

Orin paused and looked at her oddly. "If I remember right, he said that they had a silver weaving and in the center was a tiny skull with red eyes to match its owner."

Hailey thought back to the boy in the market. Was it the same ring? Orin was still looking at her, then continued on, turning back to the sea.

"The ghost pirate just stood for a long time on the deck, staring at him. Dad thought for sure it would jump over the rail and split him in two, but instead the ghost just turned and walked away and left him to die from cold and exposure.

"Out of the whole crew of fifty men, he was the only survivor. His boat broke up and sank, and the black ship just vanished into the mists as quickly as it came, leaving him alone in the water holding on to only a small section of the mast that stayed afloat."

"How terrifying. Poor Grandfather!"

"Luckily, a crew on one of the Crown patrol ships happened to see him floating in the water the next morning and brought him aboard. He tried to tell them what happened, but they didn't believe him."

He turned back to Hailey, shaking his head.

"It wasn't just the Crown, though. No one would believe him. They didn't want to hear what really happened, no matter how many times he tried to tell them."

They stood quietly for a while until Hailey asked, "Do you think the ghost pirates still roam the seas?"

"I don't know. Sometimes I wonder. Your grandfather disappeared at sea when you were a baby. I always wondered if they had anything to do with it. You see, he told me that once pirates see you, they never let you go. I don't know why he thought that. Oddly enough, his was the last ship to disappear into the mists." He looked down uncomfortably. "Maybe they finally got what they were looking for."

The mists had crept up a bit too close for either of their liking, especially given the story he'd just told. They both decided to head towards home.

They walked in silence. Hailey was lost in thought, thankful that her father had not called her out for taking the book. Instead he chose to let it go and tell her the story about the book itself and how it was meant for her anyway. After reading it, she now also knew why her mother wanted to get away from the book.

Her mind was awash with questions. Was that what they were looking for when they attacked her grandfather's ship? Or did the ghost pirates take away her grandfather for having seen them? Had the ghost pirates been after her mother, too? If so, would they do the same to her if she had the book? Or worse? If her mother had wanted to get away from it, why tell her father to get it back for her?

Orin turned to her and interrupted her thoughts. "It's been a long time since I heard anyone ask anything about pirates. What made you bring it up?"

She shook her head slightly to dispel all the questions swirling around her. She then shrugged, and while doing so, reached back and touched the edge of the book in her waistband once more.

"I don't know. Maybe it was something I read."

# CHAPTER 8

The next day was a blur of faces and bodies to get everything ready. Swarms of ladies arrived at their house just after dawn to aid and claim credit for preparation of the evening's events at the colonial mansion in the heart of town. Hailey's grandmother commanded the seemingly endless throng like a general in the field, and it was as if they were going to war with the Crown instead of hosting a welcoming party for one of its grand emissaries.

Hailey tried her best to remain hidden from her family. After their long beach walk, Orin was summoned to the Merchant's Guild House. It was late, and Hailey was asleep by the time he came back. After a long voyage such as theirs, he would normally have to meet and resolve conflicts within the guild when he returned, but the meetings were usually brief and he was home by supper time. Not this time.

Orin returned looking haggard and exhausted as the sun was beginning to peek out of the eastern sky. Hailey heard him collapse into his bed at the top of the stairs for an hour until her grandmother quickly swooped down on him. Something was amiss with the party preparations, and she

"

needed Orin to go and sort it out right away, so she harassed and pecked away at him until he finally relented and got up.

Hailey heard the two of them go downstairs and thought it the best time to sneak down and get out of sight before her grandmother could find her. Her grandmother had made her go to bed early, which told her that Hailey had a list of things she didn't want to do awaiting her downstairs. She had planned on staying up and reading the book, but her grandmother had watched over her until she doused her light and surrendered to sleep.

She took the book from under her pillow and slid it under the false bottom of her dresser. Once done, she put on her dressing gown and quietly crept down the stairs. At the bottom of the stairs, her grandmother appeared at her side as if out of thin air. Hailey flinched and stifled a yelp.

"Oh, good! You saved me the trip. Go back upstairs and get dressed, dear; we need to make our way down to the mansion."

Hailey had been caught. She didn't want to go, but she knew trying to resist was futile. From the dining room, she could hear the chattering of Rose's friends waiting on them, so she bustled back up the stairs and quickly dressed, knowing that her day would be filled with cleaning.

Grandmother Rose pattered up to Orin as he sat at the dining room table, where he was drinking a cup of coffee and reading over the lists of instructions and items needed from his mother. He didn't look up as Grandmother Rose gave him a peck on the cheek and told him goodbye. Hailey remembered that her grandmother once did the same for her not too long ago. Now that her mother was gone, the simple and doting grandmother Hailey once knew was gone, replaced with a woman determined to make up for her dead mother's absence. Grandmother Rose meant well, but she still missed the kisses and kindness all the same.

Hailey looked back with envy at her father as she joined the group of ladies as they left to go to the mansion. She wished that she could be left alone to read as well. Hailey wished she could be an observer of the storm, not caught in its fury. She had so many questions about the book. Where did it come from? What did it have to do with the ghost pirates? Was that what they were looking for when they attacked her grandfather's ship? Why did the ghost pirates want it in the first place? She had the feeling that all the answers she was looking for were in that book. She just needed to find the time and a place to hide and read it. Unfortunately, it wouldn't be happening today.

Hailey knew that there was a lot of work to be done to get the mansion ready for the party. The normally short walk to get from her house to the mansion seemed like an eternity. Every step along the way, Grandmother Rose ticked off things that would either need to be cleaned or arranged when they got there.

The mansion had stood vacant for some time; its last inhabitant a Crown overseer, had been called back to the capital just before the Cowl's Ridge incident. It had been years since anyone even thought about a replacement—there was simply no need. The Merchant's Guild paid its tithes and taxes on time. Daden's shipping had never slowed; goods flowed throughout the empire, and population growth and sentiment weren't enough to merit attention from the Crown. They were all happy and content, so it had been a surprise to them all when the decree went out that the Crown was sending them another representative.

As they walked up the stairs leading up to the grand white mansion, Grandmother Rose explained to the ladies that once she had heard the announcement in the town square, her sense of propriety and duty couldn't allow a man of such high status to arrive without a grand welcome. Hailey wondered if it wasn't simply ulterior motives. Her mind went back to the fitting the day before, as she grabbed a bucket and a mop and went to work removing the years of neglect from the mansion.

As the morning wore on, the storm of ladies began to slowly dissipate as they slipped out to prepare for the night's activities. It was just after lunchtime when Rose was satisfied enough to dismiss everyone from setting up.

Hailey and her grandmother walked home in silence. Once through the gate, Hailey followed her grandmother, and they walked the path around the main house to the small wooden-slatted kitchen house out back. A swarm of servants were coming in and out, carrying trays of foods, dancing around each other as they passed on the narrow staircase like bees in a hive.

Grandmother Rose went inside to check on the servants, making sure that every red-haired one of them was hard at work making desserts for the evening. Though the church preached that red-heads were hard workers bread for labor and to serve everyone, Rose didn't quite the trust them to do a good enough job by her standards. Hailey used the moment's distraction to try and sneak off to her room, but her grandmother caught sight of her and called out to her.

"Young lady, are you going into the house like that?"

Hailey stopped and looked down at herself. She hadn't noticed how grimy and sweaty she had become from cleaning the mansion. She looked as if she were wearing years' worth of grime and neglect.

Her grandmother came up to her, nose wrinkled.

"Honestly, Hailey. You smell awful!" Grandmother Rose took Hailey by the arm and marched her out to the bath house.

"Scrub up for the party. I'll have one of the servants bring you a fresh towel when you are done; then you can go in and get dressed."

Heated bath houses were quite the luxury in the colonies, even one as old as this one. Piping in water to homes was simple enough. As tree homes were shaped, shapers would run water lines to irrigate, so it was only natural and easy to pressurize them and tap them at various places throughout a house, but they were never heated before. To heat water for a bath, one would have to go to the cook house and boil it in a pot over a fire, an often long and backbreaking process, so most people just went for cold showers or bucket baths.

One day Orin had returned from a cargo run from the capital with a surprise—one of the magic heating boxes. Hailey didn't know how he got it or even what one would pay for such a thing; all she knew after her first warm bath was that she never wanted to take a cold bucket wash again.

Hailey entered the bath house and locked the door behind her, glad to have a moment alone, but it was only a moment. As soon as she slipped into the tub of warm water, her grandmother began to harass her through the walls.

"Now, Hailey, there will be several guests from the noble houses as well as the Governor. You don't have to socialize with them long, but I do want them to get a good look at you. There should be plenty of eligible young men your age you can socialize with."

Hailey tried to ignore her and enjoy a nice soak before being put on display again. As she'd suspected, this party wasn't about propriety or altruism after all. It was about Rose's hunt for the best husband for her granddaughter. He would have to be one Rose could brag to the ladies at the tea stand for decades to come. Since Grandmother Rose was in charge of the guest list, only the wealthiest and most ambitious men would be there. How could they say no? In the social circles, this event was like a candle to a moth. What better way to get all the rich prospects in the region to come to them than to host the arrival of the island's new governor?

Hailey settled back into the warm water, letting her ears sink below the water line to drown out her grandmother's words.

THE PARTY BEGAN EARLY in the evening, giving the guests plenty of time to be fashionably late. The colonial mansion was an oddity. It was the only building not made from a molded and shaped tree; it was instead a large white box that looked as if someone had placed it there. It was larger than most of the other houses. Daden was once the heart of the western exploration and expansion effort of the Crown. It's tree homes were larger than most of the other colonies, but this odd building was larger. It was two or three times the size of that of its neighbors. Even though the mansion was large the party spilled out to the long and lush front and back lawns for those who had tired of dancing or eaten their fill at the buffet.

Hailey felt uncomfortable in her lacy white dress, feeling as if she weren't wearing it as much as being possessed by it. it was visually stunning, complete with a beautiful red ribbon as an accent, but wearing it was torturous to her. It hugged her just enough in some places and was loose enough in others to give her the illusion of an hourglass figure. Moving was awkward, with the clinginess of the top of the dress contrasted by the breezy and flowing bell of the skirt of the dress. Hailey managed.

She was lovely, at least that was what every gentleman told her as she and her grandmother greeted them at the door. Her grandmother's response every time was the same.

"Thank you, she takes after me."

Her grandmother made every effort to introduce Hailey to every eligible bachelor, and after each one, she gave Hailey a short, whispered briefing on their status, approximately how much wealth they had, and topics to talk with them about later.

Grandmother Rose gave the impression of being more her broker than a matron in those moments, but it was to be expected. As it was taught in schools and in their primers, it was one of the main reasons people went to these events— the quest to raise one's social status and earning potential through the blessings of marriage. At least, that's how the Church decreed it.

After most of the nobles had arrived, Hailey seized the opportunity to excuse herself from her hostess duties under the guise of going to talk to one of the bachelors. Hailey's grandmother approved of her prudence, noting that most of the others coming in weren't much of an advancement for her in wealth, status, or looks, and sent her on her way.

Looking around the party, Hailey concluded it had proved to be an immense success, but the crowd seemed restless. There were several heads of guilds, wealthy merchants by the score, and nobles from all across the island, but the bishop had yet to arrive.

Hailey made her way over to the buffet table on the side of the great room. Talking with so many young nobles and pretending to laugh at their stale jokes made her throat dry. She had done her best, though, and the times she saw her grandmother pass by to check on her, Rose was beaming.

"Hailey, I need to talk to you." Hailey felt a hand on her shoulder and turned to see her father standing beside her. She was surprised to see him. Before the party started he had disappeared, called away to the Merchant's Guild on an urgent matter.

Before she could respond, someone dressed in the scarlet

of the Royal Guard blasted a horn from the door, demanding everyone's attention. The crowd pressed to the door, all hoping to be the first to greet one of the highest representatives of the Church of the Ancestors. Hailey's grandmother may have been old, even ancient by some standards, but she was not without strength or motivation. She plowed her way through the pack of well-wishers and arrived at the threshold of the door just in time to greet the bishop.

Hailey and her father watched mutely. Neither of them could get a look at him through the crush of the crowd. Hailey hoped the distraction would last just a bit longer, but her father would not wait. He turned her away from the crowds and spoke in a low voice.

"Hailey, where is it? Is it here?"

Her mind flashed instantly to the book. She had hidden it in her room before the party, unable to keep it on her in such a form-fitting dress. Her father had gone through her room in the past, she was sure of it, but he had yet to find her secret hiding place.

"Is w-w-what here?" she stammered.

"You know what. The *book*." He glared at her.

A new voice, one she had never heard before, came from directly behind them.

"Books? Oh, I simply love books!"

She turned to see her grandmother standing on the arm of a tall, slender man with high cheekbones and a light brown complexion. He was dressed in a dark, rich blue jacket and pants accented with woven gold on the sleeves and collar. It was the dapper man she had seen the day before, both in the market as well as on the boat. Not only was he wearing the same outfit, he still held that creepy smile with almost too many teeth.

He smiled at Orin and said, "So do you, from what I hear." He cocked his head at Orin, leaning in. "At least, that's what

Captain Langen tells me!" And then he winked mischievously at him.

"Bishop Graver, this is my son, Orin Heartstone, and my young granddaughter, Hailey," Rose said proudly.

Orin and Hailey stood stunned. Rose cleared her throat and raised her eyebrows at them to snap them out of it as the bishop stood in front of them, still grinning. Orin gave a slight bow and Hailey gave a curtsey. The bishop's gaze, still locked on Orin, then shifted to Hailey, giving her the impression of a lighthouse beacon swiveling to catch her in its beam. She tried to avoid his eyes, but he stepped closer to her.

"Yes, a lovely young lady!"

He looked at her for a long moment. Almost too long. Hailey felt as though he were examining her instead of greeting her. Suddenly and quickly, he pivoted to her grandmother, saying, "She must take after you, naturally!" He had more than just a little twinkle in his eye when he said it. Having her line stolen, Rose could only force a laugh and nod her agreement.

Graver swiveled his attention back to Hailey, taking her by the hand. She stood trapped, caught in a grip that was just gentle enough but certainly firm. His eyes never left her face, as if he were searching for something.

"Bishop Jacob Graver, at your service." He bowed to her. Hailey blushed and didn't know what to do, so she looked to her grandmother for guidance. Rose raised her eyebrow at Hailey and mouthed the words, "Pleased to meet you" at her.

"Pleased to meet you?" It came out like a question, though Hailey didn't intend it to.

The bishop smiled brightly and let her hand go as he straightened up.

"The pleasure is all mine!" He smiled at her with his toothy grin, making Hailey feel uncomfortable. The man was a bishop of the Church of the Ancestors, one of the leaders of faith and education. They were the embodiment of propriety and one of the most powerful allies the Crown had ever known. The Crown controlled the magic and the markets, and the Church controlled the printing of books and the faith of the flock. The marriage between the two powers signaled the consolidation of the Queen's ambitions to control the hearts and minds of her subjects.

Though this man was supposed to be a shepherd to the faithful, she didn't like the way the bishop looked at her. She didn't feel like a member of the flock. She felt like prey.

"Back to books," he said, addressing Orin. "I know you are quite the fan of literature. Good taste, mind you. I'm sure that you have passed on that passion to your daughter. In fact, just yesterday I saw her in the market reading when I went to have tea."

Hailey's grandmother looked horrified. "Sir, you astonish me! I had no idea you had arrived! Had I known, I would have welcomed you sooner!"

"Don't trouble yourself, madam. I didn't let anyone know I was here. I like to walk around in the crowd unnoticed. It lets me see things more clearly, see how things are. I had to tip my hat to your young daughter yesterday," he said, turning his head back to Orin, addressing him but still facing the rest of his body toward Hailey. "She was so engrossed in reading she hardly noticed anything around her. It was only by chance that she looked up and saw me." He turned to Hailey. "So what book had you so fascinated?"

Hailey had to think fast. Something in his gaze told her that he knew something, and she was in great danger. She couldn't break eye contact with him, and she felt her father's and grandmother's eyes on her.

She said the only thing she could think of.

"I was reading my primer."

It was a response that seemed to surprise both her father as well as Bishop Graver.

She forced her shoulders into a slight slump. If she was going to sell this, she would have to play the part well. She let her cheeks drop as her smile faded. She let her body cringe slightly as she broke her gaze with Bishop Graver and looked at her grandmother as she spoke.

"I was supposed to read my primer on my trip, but I didn't. I was trying to catch up before the party." She lowered her head to her grandmother as if to apologize. She hadn't completely lied, but the discomfort she displayed was real. She didn't like to tell a lie, even a little lie, but in this case she had to.

"I see. Good to see a keen interest in such an important book. It gives a wondrous comfort. Unfortunately, in my haste to get here I forgot mine in the palace in the capitol. Perhaps I can borrow yours?"

Hailey froze. The Church printed the primers and taught from them on a daily basis in their schools and churches. He had access to any number of primers. Why would he want hers?

She could see it in his searching eyes. This man didn't want her primer. He was after the book. A cold chill hit her as she realized that she had to do everything she could to be sure he didn't get it.

The Crown had too much power. It was a power they wielded like a hammer against any who would stand against them. At first they used their magics to decimate those who resisted their order, but that had changed when the Veiled Queen took the throne. Hailey knew from her father's books that, after taking the throne from her late husband, the Queen learned to control the people through a more subtle and insidious method.

The Crown gave the colonies magic devices that

controlled everything keeping the towns going. The lights, weather forecasters, miracle medicines, even the devices that brought water into their homes were all theirs and under their contol. It was a wonderful boon to the colonies, and they flourished because of it, but it all came with a price. If you displeased the Crown in any way, they would remind you of life before their magics, forcing you to live like a primitive. The Crown no longer had to threaten to attack and invade the colonies as they had 100 years ago; all they had to do was withdraw their magics, and the people would beg them to come back.

She knew then that her book had power. It had a raw, living power the likes of which the world had never seen. It gave the user an Ancestor-sized view of their living world and hinted at treasures beyond imagining. The idea of giving this over to the Crown bothered her more than any amount of lying. She couldn't let another powerful tool fall into the Queen's clutches. She had heard rumors of the terrible things the Queen would do to people. Especially with magic tools. There were even rumors that she was somehow involved in the incident at Cowl's Ridge.

Her father picked up on her distress and leapt into the conversation.

"It was her mother's," he said, and Rose shot him a look of surprise, but didn't say anything. "It was passed down to her after her mother died at Cowl's Ridge. We thought it would be a good way to bring her closer to her mom."

At the mention of Cowl's Ridge, the bishop wisely did not reply. He simply allowed the moment of gravity to settle and, after a slight pause, carried the conversation away from the topic.

"Ah. How unfortunate. Well, no bother. It's a fine thing when a young lady carries on tradition and decides to take an interest in the teachings of the Ancestors on proper etiquette," he said, then took another tack. "Perhaps one day you will join me during one of my private tea parties?"

Hailey's grandmother gasped in surprise.

He continued. "I usually host a small reading circle with a few select people. Granted, the books aren't as engrossing as the primer, but we manage." He tried to sound casual. "I can send you an invitation the next time we get together, if you like."

Hailey's grandmother, anxious to take back control of the situation, leapt in.

"She would be delighted!" she said, positively beaming at the bishop. She hadn't quite gotten his attention away from Hailey, so she gently turned him towards her son.

"Now, Bishop…"

He turned to her and playfully said to her. "Oh, please, call me Jacob."

She blushed and tittered, "Oh, well, yes, Jacob. My son, Orin, is the head of the Merchant's Guild here in Daden. Being that you are the chief Crown representative, I am sure that you two have much to discuss."

The bishop turned and began to speak with Orin, and Hailey took that as her cue to go. She left the two men to their conversation, her grandmother hovering and holding back the line of people who wanted to see the bishop and shooing away anyone who tried to interrupt.

Hailey had to get to the book. She had to check on it. She had to be sure it was safe. It was a compulsion, like a compass that pointed her to it.

If Bishop Graver really knew she had the book, it would only be a matter of time before Crown troops would come to search their house, as they had the *Arrow*. She had to make sure it was safe. She could still feel the bishop's eyes following her as she snaked her way through the crowd, so she avoided going out the main door and slipped out through the pantry and into the backyard. There were a few people on the lawn, but they were so engrossed in their conversations they took little notice of her.

She slipped around the hedges that encircled the mansion and made her way down the empty streets back to her home.

There were no lights on in the house, and she knew the doors would be locked, so she made her way around the large tree. After checking to make sure no one was watching, Hailey kicked off her shoes and started to climb. She was just as nimble making her way up the tree as she had been on the rigging, but this time she had to take her time getting up the tree because of her dress. She didn't want to have to suffer her grandmother's wrath for getting it dirty or ripped, so she tried her best to scale the tree branches without getting anything on the dress. As she climbed the branches, she couldn't help but feel as though there were eyes upon her. She reached the window, climbed inside, and looked back to see if anyone had seen her.

Satisfied no one was there, she closed the window behind her. She padded across the room and quietly turned the lock on her door. She touched the light globe in the wall, and it began to fill the room with a soft glow. She could see the symbol of the Crown and Veil at the base, mildly glowing its constant reminder of whom the light came from.

She slipped out of her dress and put on a simple white shirt and tan long shorts before she went to retrieve the book from its hiding place.

Hailey hoped it would be hours before either her father or grandmother noticed she wasn't at the party anymore, being so tied up with the bishop and all of the guests. She needed the time alone to figure out what to do next.

She had to consult the book.

# CHAPTER 9

*H*er mind raced as she knelt before her dresser and dove her hands beneath it to recover the book. It was still there. Simply touching it gave her a slight sense of relief. The book seemed to know what was going on. Maybe it could tell her what to do? She rocked back on her knees and pulled it out. It was as if the skull were looking right up at her.

The latches along the sides of the book clicked open as she pulled the book closer. She rolled off her legs and sat on the floor, stretching out and leaning against her bed, and opened the book in her lap. She stared at the blank page and waited for it to tell her something, anything, to fix the situation. The page blankly stared back at her.

The book seemed to have a hold on her, was compelling her to do something. She started to wonder if her will was her own anymore.

Hailey sat and questioned her life. She wondered if she had ever truly done anything for herself, or had she just been putting on an act for everyone? She always did what she was told without question, whether she wanted to or not. She felt compelled to make everyone happy, especially since her mother had died.

And here she was again, wanting someone to tell her what to do. Should she give the book to her dad and let him worry about it? Should she give it to the bishop so he would leave her alone? Maybe she could throw it in the sea and hope the pirates got it?

She wanted to throw the book in the trash and be done with it, but something told her that she would only fish it out. She could give it back to her dad, but then the Crown would be after him as well. All she wanted to do was be free, free from all of it. Free from the book, her grandmother, growing up, the incessant need to please everyone. She wanted to be free from all of it. She just wanted to live her life how she wanted to.

A hole in her soul the shape of her mom ached. She wished she could see her, talk to her. She would have known what to do.

She shook the book in frustration and asked it through clenched teeth, "What am I supposed to do?"

Words bubbled up on the page.

***BE READY***
***THEY KNOW***

The words instantly sent her from being simply afraid into full-blown panic. She began to sweat and shake as she held the book.

"What?" She fought the urge to scream at it and forced a whisper. "Who are they and what do they know?"

***THE BISHOP***

*THE QUEEN.*
*THEY KNOW YOU HAVE THE BOOK.*
*THEY KNOW YOU CAN OPEN IT.*
*THEY WILL COME FOR YOU, HAILEY.*
*IT WON'T END WELL.*

Hailey couldn't help but gulp at the last line. Wouldn't end well? Also, the book knew that Bishop Graver had seen her with the book. How was that possible? A few seconds ago she had just wanted wanted to live her own life, now she wanted more than ever for someone to tell her what to do. She found herself wishing she'd waited for her father to come home with her. She was having a hard time controlling her breathing. She started to rock back and forth while anxiously clutching at the book and gritting her teeth.

"This isn't happening. This isn't happening." Over and over she repeated the words like a chant to convince herself, but it didn't work.

The book cleared its pages and responded.

**HAILEY, THIS IS HAPPENING**

Hailey could have sworn she heard the book sigh.

*ARE YOU WAITING FOR ME TO TELL YOU WHAT TO DO?*

"Yes." She was ashamed to admit it.

*EMBRACE YOUR FATE. YOU ARE THE NAVIGATOR,*
*AFTER ALL.*
*YOU MUST GO OUT TO SEA AND MEET THE PIRATES.*
*NOW*
*BEFORE THE CROWN COMES TO GET YOU.*

Now? In the middle of the night? There were no boats sailing from the harbor at that hour. How could seeking out the pirates be better than being taken by the Crown?

Again, reading her thoughts, the book responded.

### *YOU MAY LIVE SLIGHTLY LONGER IF YOU DO.*

The words were of no comfort to her. The word "slightly" seemed to burn itself in her mind before the pages cleared, and in even larger letters, more words appeared.

### *HIDE ME! SOMEONE IS COMING*

She looked up and snapped the book shut. She barely heard the soft creak of someone coming up the stairs. Probably her grandmother coming to check and see where she had gotten off to. The woman not only watched her like a hawk, she was as silent as one, too. Hailey slid the book back under the dresser and quickly stood to touch the light globe again, bringing the room into darkness. She slid under the covers just as someone began to work at the lock on the door.

Though she kept her eyes shut, Hailey could feel the light from the open door on her face. She could hear the soft nasal breathing of her grandmother as she stood over her.

"Oh, child," she whispered softly to herself. "I wish I could do more for you."

What Hailey wished her grandmother could do for her at that moment was to leave so she could listen to the book and make her escape, but it was not to be. Rose stood in the doorway, sighing and looking over her, and Hailey heard her leave. Then to Hailey's horror, she heard the soft commotion of a chair being brought in. Rose set it down gently, and there was a series of quiet creaks as she settled in next to the bed. Hailey was trapped in the room. She tried to wait her grandmother out, but Rose would not leave.

Hailey eventually gave up and went to sleep, hoping she could slip away in the morning.

# CHAPTER 10

*H*ailey's eyes flew open, and she sat up in fear as her grandmother burst into the room. Had she slept at all? She felt as though she had only just closed her eyes.

"Get up, child! I have wonderful news."

Her grandmother moved about the room, opening the shutters to let the light in; then she shuffled to the tall closet next to Hailey's dresser and began looking through the dresses.

The light was dim and warm, telling Hailey that it was early in the morning, and the sun was still relatively low in the sky. It had been late already when Hailey snuck away from the party. She wondered if her grandmother had slept at all or if she had stayed up through the night.

Rose came over to her bedside and laid a dress on the covers.

"You, my dear, must have made quite the impression last night!"

Hailey squinted up at her, trying to follow. "What do you mean?"

"You received a letter first thing this morning from the bishop." Her grandmother looked as if she could hardly contain herself. "He's invited us to a royal tea!" Her grandmother's smile wilted a little at Hailey's expression. Instead of being full of elation, it was tense with fear.

"Now, Hailey, there's no need to be like that." Her grandmother crossed the floor and opened another cabinet to look for matching shoes. "Naturally I accepted the invitation right away. They will send a coach over shortly to pick us up."

Hailey kicked off the covers and stood to protest, but her grandmother cut her off.

"No time to delay. Be sure to clean up and get dressed." And with that she exited the room, closing the door behind her.

Hailey grumbled in frustration. Her grandmother's good intentions had delivered her right into the Crown's hands. She sat on the bed and sighed. What would the book say?

She knew what the book had said the night before. It told her that she was in danger and the only way out of this mess was to find the pirates. If that was the case, she would have to get to the docks.

She pulled back the cover and looked at the dress her grandmother had picked out for her. It was made of a light yellow fabric with small white flowers sewn on. Grandmother Rose had bought it for her before she left with her father for Baron's Bay. Hailey's teenage mind thought it made her look too much like a little girl. It made her look like another dress-up doll to play with.

Like many of the outfits her grandmother had bought her before, it came with a porcelain doll with the same outfit. It was an extra expense that her grandmother thought would bring Hailey some kind of joy. After all, she was her only granddaughter, and in a way, the little girl she had never had herself. She did it out of love; Hailey knew that. But had Rose ever paid attention, she would have seen the layer of dust on the other dolls she had gotten for her in the past, as they sat quietly and untouched on the shelves Hailey's grandmother had so carefully shaped out of the tree to line Hailey's walls.

The new doll looked out at her from the glass case in which it was trapped, along with several others. The dolls meant that Hailey didn't need to look at her wardrobe; she had a miniature glass display of all of her outfits. She often thought her grandmother wanted her to be just like those tiny dolls. Tiny dolls with their perfect clothes, perfect hair, with perfect made-up tan faces who looked out at the world through dead empty eyes calmly waiting for someone to control them.

Hailey decided it best to put on the dress over her shorts and shirt, so she could quickly change later if she needed to. She let down her hair and brushed it out, then worked it back into her usual sea braid. Hailey knew that her grandmother would not approve, but considering that she was wearing the dress her grandmother chose, Hailey didn't think Grandmother Rose would fight her too much.

She made one last check to verify that the book still remained in its hiding spot. It was still there. She couldn't understand the anxiety she felt by its absence, like a feeling gnawing at her to pick it up. That she had too touch it, to read it right away. She wished she had time to sit and read it, but between her grandmother and the gurgling of her stomach, she had to get to breakfast. Besides, bringing a contraband book to a Crown function was surely a recipe for a hanging, especially since the bishop was after it.

Her stomach growled loudly once again, so she stepped away from the dresser, quickly put on her shoes, and made her way to the door. Driven by hunger , she trotted down the stairs that lined the wall of the home. On the way down, she looked over the vast open space that was the entrance and living room, and she saw it was empty save for a pack of servants doing their morning work. The handful of servants, all with the flaming red hair of the servant class, picked up their pace of morning work when they caught sight of Hailey. She had never reprimanded them before, but Hailey had seen her grandmother do so dozens of times. In their minds, she must be just as bossy by association. They must have concluded that if her grandmother scolded them, Hailey in time would do so as well. Hailey shook her head at the thought.

At the bottom of the stairs, she decided that everyone must be in the dining room and crossed towards the back of the house. Her stomach continued to growl.

Entering the formal dining room, she saw that it was also empty. No one sat at the large wooden table in the center of the room. She knew that there was only one other place they could all be gathered for breakfast. She made her way to the kitchen house.

Inside, there was a small table to the side. The table had already seen its first morning visitor, for a folded *Morning Tidelands* news sheet and an empty coffee mug rested at one of the empty settings on the small table. Her father must have already gone. Hailey had hoped he would be there so she could tell him what the book had said. She needed to get his advice, even tell her what to do.

Grandmother Rose descended the stairs of the kitchen, a young servant in tow, carrying a cast iron skillet sizzling with eggs and bacon. The young servant girl set the pan on the table's trivet and removed her gloves, bowed slightly to Grandmother Rose, and hustled back into the kitchen.

"Please, eat. They may be serving finger food at the tea, but I don't want you to arrive at the bishop's party on an empty stomach. Heaven forbid people see how much you really eat." She chuckled to herself as she pulled up a seat.

Hailey pounced on the eggs and bacon, scooping as much as she could on her plate. She hadn't had much to eat before or during the party, and she found herself so ravenous that she thought she could eat her weight in eggs.

"Where's Dad?" Hailey asked around a mouthful of eggs. Grandmother Rose gave her a withering look.

"Now, Hailey, I don't want you to display such poor manners today. It will be the death of me." She sighed. "Your father went out early to talk with a few members of the guild. He should be back by the time you return from the tea. He mentioned that he wanted to talk to you about something."

Hailey paused briefly in her inhalation of her breakfast. She remembered the look in her father's eyes at the party when he asked about the book. There must be something important going on, and it involved the guild as well as the Crown.

The moment she finished the last bite on her plate, her grandmother took the plate and got up and went to the kitchen to hand the dish to a servant. Returning to the table, she stood over Hailey.

"Well, let me look at you." Hailey stood, and her grandmother looked her over and tsked to herself about Hailey's obviously poor choice in hairstyles. It would have to do. She didn't have time to do anything else.

From the doorway of the house, one of the servants, this one tall and wide with his long hair pulled into a bun, stood and waited for Grandmother Rose to notice him. Hailey recognized him as the family groundsman, one of their handful of servants.

"Yes, what is it?" Rose called out to him.

The servant's voice was a deep baritone that sounded like a low church bell as he announced across the courtyard, "Crown emissary to see you, ma'am."

Rose took a step towards the house to go and greet the emissary, but the sound of hard boots on wooden floors behind the groundsman made her stop.

The tall servant stepped aside, and a man wearing the royal red of a Crown officer stepped forward. His features were chiseled and his complexion slightly darker, betraying his time in outdoor service. This man was more marine than emissary.

"I am here to escort Miss Hailey Heartstone to the mansion." His body language offered more command than conversation.

"Excellent, let us be on our way." Grandmother Rose made a step forward, but was halted by a sharp hand gesture from the emissary.

"My orders are to escort Miss Heartstone, and Miss Heartstone alone, to the colonial mansion."

"This cannot be! You don't expect me to send my only granddaughter off to a formal function unaccompanied!"

"Is it her safety that you are concerned about?" He cocked an eyebrow at her, the corners of his mouth raising slightly.

"Not at all. I am just concerned that it is her first formal event, that is all. She might not know to handle the social situation properly without my guidance—"

The man tilted his head and looked at her questioningly while raising an eyebrow. His face seemed to grow even darker.

"Are you saying that you are a better teacher of manners and decorum than one of the heads of the almighty Church of the Ancestors?"

Hailey could tell Grandmother Rose was not going to win

this one. Even though he was only an emissary—if she were to believe that—he still wore the royal red of the Crown. The royal red was not just a symbol of nobility, but a warning of the price to those who questioned the Crown. A blood red price.

Hailey could see the defeat registering on Grandmother Rose's face and her self-assurance deflating.

"Not at all, good sir. Please forgive me."

The man nodded, and Rose turned to Hailey, put her hands on her shoulders, and tried to give her best smile. The trepidation in her eyes was hard for Hailey to miss. Hailey could see that her concern for letting Hailey go wasn't just the decorum; it was for her safety. Stories about Crown representatives behaving badly or marrying off the lower classes to nobles had been common gossip around the tea carts for years. Grandmother Rose feared that this might be such an occasion.

For all of Grandmother Rose's rigidity, Hailey knew that there was nothing but softness in her grandmother's heart for her. Her being so hard on Hailey was her way of showing her love to her, in her own peculiar way. Rose demanded better of her because she could see better in Hailey. In that moment, Hailey realized just how much her grandmother really loved her.

The two looked at each other a long moment, as if they were saying a silent last goodbye. Grandmother Rose broke the silence with a sigh.

"Well, you better get going. I don't want you to be late."

Hailey nodded and hugged her grandmother, which took Rose by surprise. It was the first time either of them could recall hugging one another in some time.

Her grandmother whispered to her. "Be careful."

"I will."

Grandmother Rose quickly released her, nodded at the emissary, and scooted to the kitchen house, trying to hide the look of concern on her face.

"Come back to us soon, dear." She tried to smile a bit.

Hailey could only nod briskly and turned and walked over to the emissary, who gave a slight bow and motioned for her to go ahead of him.

They went through the interior of the tree house and out the side door. A large coach awaited them, drawn by two great steel horses. The emissary opened the door, helped her into the carriage, and closed the door. A muted ping and thump told Hailey that the door had locked behind her. The emissary took his seat on top of the carriage, and with a lurch, the coach rolled out onto the crowded morning streets.

THE STREETS WERE CROWDED, slowing the progress of the carriage on its route to the mansion. Crowds crested around the steel horses like water on the prow of a ship; people parted and ebbed back in their wake. She had thought about picking the lock and running, but the emissary would surely see her leaving and stop her. She had to bide her time and hope that something came up that she could take advantage of to get away. If the book was right, she was riding into danger.

Alone in the carriage, Hailey chose to pass the time looking out the window. She had never been in a carriage before and was disappointed by the interior. Though it was soft and luxurious, it was rather plain. There was nothing to catch her eye, just simple silk benches and padded walls. Outside the carriage at least offered her something to look at. She thought about her situation, her eyes following the flow of people around the square as they passed, though she could not enjoy the sights, sounds, and smells of the town's open markets as she had before.

Her thoughts swirled about with the grim possibilities of what lay ahead. She could be either be hanged for contraband or be killed by ghosts. Either way, it would end badly for her and her father. But he was the one who had acquired the book in the first place and lied to a Crown captain about it. Maybe if she threw herself on the mercy of the Crown, they would spare her father?

Her gaze followed the eddy of people to the vendor carts where she'd sat the day before. She looked around at the tables, half expecting to see Bishop Graver watching her once again, but the tables were mostly empty. Nor did she see that boy from the day before. She was alone.

Just outside of the square, the carriage lurched to a halt. The crowds seemed to pause around them. Hailey leaned out of the window to see what was going on.

"Cart overturned," she overheard someone say. This was it. Should she want to get away, this would be her best and only chance.

Hailey took a hairpin out and worked the lock, thinking with some regret that lock picking was what got her into this trouble in the first place. The door opened with a pop, and she gingerly stepped down onto the cobblestones, careful to see if the emissary noticed. He was not on top of the carriage as he had been before. He was at the overturned cart, trying to get people together to help right the large cart blocking their way. She stepped into the crowd, not sure what she was going to do.

Halfway between the docks and the colonial mansion, she was caught in indecision. Should she listen to the book and go to the docks and stow away on the first ship out of port?

Should she do the proper thing and go back to the carriage and attend the tea? Her grandmother wouldn't have let her go alone, if she hadn't thought Hailey was safe, would she? Was her life in as much danger going to the mansion as it would be taking her chances with the ghost pirates? Both decisions held such grim uncertainties that she didn't know what to do. Neither direction looked as though it would end well for her.

She looked down the lane to the market and the docks. The flowing river of people made her feel as though she were standing at the head of the waterfall. It gave her comfort watching the throngs of humanity flow to and fro, swept up and carried along at a pace not of their making.

She stood on the edge of the crowd of people waiting for the cart to be moved. Looking around, she couldn't see the emissary, but she did see the current of people flowing towards the docks and felt the slight pull of their wake. She was tempted to go with the flow and drift away, but she wasn't sure she should. She scanned the crowd, hoping there was someone, something, to tell her what to do.

Hailey looked up the lane, past the overturned cart, and saw the towering colonial mansion, its impossibly white face with large dark windows like eyes watching her. It looked out of place. It was something artificial in a world of green and living homes and shops. It made of a white stone not found anywhere on the island. The building reminded Hailey of a giant tooth piercing up though the green grass. One of the many fangs of the crown that bit into the lands of the colonies. It stood as yet another reminder of the power of the Queen.

Inside were housed impossible magics that defied the mind. There were mirrors that people could use to talk to each other in other lands and metal men, like the horses, that moved around as servants. Hailey had seen magic items all over the mansion when she had cleaned it the day before. She did her best to clean around them. At one point she had stumbled into the storeroom where the metal men stood, silently waiting, their dark eyes looking at her in unblinking sleep. The sight unnerved Hailey so much, she bolted from the room.

She was so engrossed in the memory that she jumped back startled as a man in front of her turned, cleared his throat, and looked at her. It was the young man she'd seen in the market, the one she'd come to think of as beautiful. He stood motionless, his sand-colored eyes looking at her intensely.

"I wouldn't go in there," he said, thumbing over his shoulder towards the mansion. His voice was a bit deeper than she had expected. His accent was a little crude, but understandable. She couldn't quite place it, but it sounded a little like that of someone from the western isles, like Iconen or one of the smaller isles that surrounded it.

She looked him over. He was taller than she remembered, but only slightly. He was probably around her age, or perhaps a little older. She didn't notice much about most boys her age, but this one, this one was different. He stood out in her mind like a drop of color on an otherwise black and white canvas.

He stood, arms folded, and she could see the knots of muscles in his forearms merging into chiseled biceps, which told her that he led a life of labor. His tan skin tone and longish hair told her it was a life at sea. Whoever he was, she didn't mind looking at him at all.

He grew impatient and he moved towards her and unfolded his arms. "You are in danger. We must go."

As he advanced, Hailey took a step back from him and put her arms up.

The young man stopped.

"Look, we don't have much time, we need to go!"

He advanced again, and she took another step back. The boy then vanished into the crowd that swirled around them. She took a couple of quick steps forward, scanning the sea of faces, but none were familiar. None of the people she could see had those odd pale eyes.

Behind her stood the red-coated emissary, wiping the sweat off his face with a handkerchief. Startled to see her out of the carriage, he stepped to her quickly.

"I don't know how you got out, but it's time to go, ma'am."

He motioned her back to the carriage, holding open the door, but she didn't move. She had missed her chance to get away, lost in indecision, and when the help she'd hoped for arrived, she let it slip away.

She stood for a long moment, looking at the gray crowd swirling down the now freed lanes and around the imposing white block that was the colonial mansion. She looked up into its dark windows bordered by blood red curtains and tried not to imagine the bishop standing there. Watching. Waiting.

She thought for a moment about turning and running, losing the emissary in the crowds and making her way to the first ship she could find, but again her fate would be unknown. Worst of all, it would come back to her father and possibly even her grandmother. What would happen to them if she ran now?

She looked around one last time. Hailey hoped the young man would appear from the crowd again and stop her, but he did not. There was nothing to stop her from climbing back into the carriage, and the door closed behind her with a click of finality. The carriage lurched forward and brought her up the streets to the long carriage path to the front of the colonial mansion.

They stopped at the front stairs, and the carriage door opened. Hailey looked up the long flight of stairs to the mansion, as a pair of guards began to pull open the massive iron front doors. Its dark entrance reminded Hailey of a gaping maw. She climbed the stairs alone, passed the guards, and let the building swallow her whole.

Once her eyes adjusted to the dimness, Hailey saw she was greeted by a silent servant at the doorway, who escorted her down the hallway. The lit orbs that lined the walls seemed to bleed their light into the dark, rich, red-and-gold wallpaper that adorned the walls.

From the shadows, the portraits of past Crown officials stood in silent formation along the hallway, watching her progression. Kings, queens, and bishops all eyed her as she warily made her way down the hall. The wigged and petticoated manservant plodded mindlessly down the hallway, never looking back at her. He turned the corner abruptly, expecting her to follow.

They stopped as the servant opened a great, dark wooden door with a flourish and stepped through. Hailey paused for a moment to take in the room. It was a grand ballroom, lightly colored in whites and linens and lined with windows looking out over the lawns. There were crystal chandeliers that hung low, their warm light brightening the room like sunlight. With the lush and long green carpeting underfoot, the room reminded Hailey of an outdoor garden party, though it was plain to see that they were indoors.

There were dozens of round tables, each one set with fine china and elegant silverware. In the center of each table was a small crystal vase holding fresh flowers. It was a beautiful scene, although a barren one, for there was no one in the room save her and the servant who had advanced to a table at the other end of the ballroom.

Hailey strode to catch up, and when the servant mechanically pulled back her chair and stood waiting to place her, Hailey froze. She remembered the face, and more importantly, the eyes. It was one of the mechanical servants she had stumbled across in the storeroom; their empty eyes had stared out at her from the dark and given her such a fright. This automaton didn't look at her; it didn't need to. It performed its function silently and efficiently, its dark, unblinking eyes staring mindlessly ahead, waiting for her to approach and be seated.

Looking around the empty room, Hailey wondered if she was too early for the party. She didn't think she was. If anything, the traffic had made her seem to be more than fashionably late, bordering on rude. There should have been at least a couple of people. Hailey had been subjected to several tea parties by her grandmother, and there were always at least a few people there early. And this was a high tea, with a bishop of the Church; she expected the room to be filled to the brim, not empty.

She thought of the book and the young man's warnings. If this was some kind of trap, why would they go to all of this trouble? They could have just taken her at the door or even at her home that morning. Something wasn't right.

The voice of her grandmother sounded in her head, telling her that she was being rude making the servant—even if it was a mechanical one—wait as she stood pondering. She hurried to catch up and join the automaton servant, who blankly stood waiting. Once seated, the servant wordlessly left her to the silence of the great room.

Hailey was startled when there was a crash and clang as the servant door opened, and a teacart rattled towards her. Pushing the cart was a rather diminutive red-haired servant girl dressed in a formal black dress bordered in white lace. The cart was brimming full of items and crowned with a large and elaborate teapot.

Hailey tried unsuccessfully to catch the servant's eye as she came up to the table. Hailey knew that decorum dictated that the servants were never to talk to the guests, but she hoped that she could at least get some kind of an answer out of the servant. Perhaps she'd been escorted into the wrong ballroom?

Hailey leaned over to her, trying to catch her attention.

"Excuse me, am I early?"

The servant ignored Hailey and went about arranging the tray of goods. Her motions were almost as rigid and silent as the automaton's. Hailey tried again to catch the servant's eye, but she blankly focused on the task at hand. Once she was done she swiftly departed, going back through the hidden door she had come out of.

Hailey sat looking everything over. There was enough food on the tea tray to serve several dozen people. There was a tower of baked pastries, finger foods, various meats and cheeses, and jewel-like cookies topped with various fruit spreads. The small rolling feast was much more lavish than the simple finger food her grandmother's friends had prepared for the party the night before and would have satisfied even the most ravenous of appetites.

Hailey was tempted to load up a plate full of sweets as dessert for her earlier breakfast, but the combination of the manners that her grandmother instilled in her and the looming dread of the event curtailed her sweet tooth for the moment.

Behind her, she heard the great wooden door that she had been led through earlier creak open, followed by the sounds of footsteps making their way up the carpet towards her. Her grandmother, a consummate proponent of decorum, had preached at her that a lady never turns around in her chair and waits until she is addressed to turn. Her father, a merchant and the veteran of many a tavern brawl, had taught her to never sit with her back to the door unless she couldn't help it. She wished she had listened more to her father than her grandmother at that moment.

Hailey felt her back go more rigid as the footsteps came closer. The steps stopped right behind her, and she fought the urge to turn, partly out of training and partly out of fear. Though the pause was only for a moment, it felt like an hour. Finally, two figures rounded the table, and Hailey could see that behind the metal servant strode the slim and gangly figure of Bishop Graver. The automaton pulled back the chair and sat Bishop Graver mechanically. Once done, it turned and promptly made its way to the servant's door.

"Hello, Hailey, good of you to come!" He smiled broadly at her and bowed his head in greeting. She stuttered for a moment, then thanked him for the invitation, and bowed her head in return.

"Such delightful manners. Your grandmother has taught you well." His smile didn't fade.

Again she thanked him and blushed slightly. She thought to herself that if her grandmother were there to witness her decidedly less-than-delightful manners, she would have fainted dead on the floor.

Bishop Graver let his long stork-like body relax casually into the arms of the chair, an action that seemed to deflate the formality of the occasion quite a bit. Hailey let herself relax slightly, though she still watched him carefully.

He had changed from his attire the night before. He wore the dark purple long coat and the epaulets of the vestry, something Hailey had not expected. It was unusual enough for a Crown official, especially a male bachelor, to host a formal tea. That was something they usually left to subordinate female volunteers to host. Of course they would show up and make an appearance, but they would never stay around long enough to mingle with anyone. This man took the time not only to appear, but to host and dress for the occasion. To Hailey it was an impressive sight. No matter how casual the man tried to be, his formal attire still gave the air of regality and make Hailey feel completely out of her depth.

Hailey eyed the bishop quietly as he reached his long slender arms over to the tea set. He motioned for her to give him her cup. Taking it, he filled the fine china cup with perfect balance and grace, not spilling a drop. At that moment, Hailey wasn't sure her hands would have been as steady.

He flashed one of his wide grins at her that made her think of how a fish must feel when a shark circled. She watched him intently, as though he were going to leap across the table and bite her. Noting her reaction, the bishop reined in his smile slightly.

He offered her the milk and sugar, and Hailey took both; then he settled in to fix his own cup. Satisfied, he took a sip. Hailey looked at him, surprised.

"Won't there be anyone else joining us?" she asked.

"No, I wanted this meeting to be between the two of us."

She looked around the large room, then looked back at the bishop. Reading her look, he replied, "Yes, well, it wouldn't be a formal tea without formal settings, would it?"

He leaned back slowly in his chair and looked at her from over his steaming cup for a long moment, then quickly sat forward and placed his tea on the table. Hailey reflexively sat back as if to give the tall figure more room or more distance across the table.

Noting her reaction, Bishop Graver reached over to the teacart and snared one of the small sugar cookies with a dollop of some kind of fruit jam on it. He broke the awkward silence that had been building in those few moments and gave her an inviting look.

"You simply must try these; they truly are delightful."

He offered the plate of them to Hailey, who took a couple and placed them on her plate. Bishop Graver took a bite of his cookie and savored it.

"Mmmm, yes, delightful. I have to say, in all of my travels, this place has the best pastries. It's the ingredients, you know. Fresh off the boat. It's always better when things come to you instead of your going to it." He contemplated his cookie again then glanced at her.

"You are quite the traveler yourself, aren't you?"

Hailey was confused. She didn't know what to say. He continued.

"I mean, you travel quite a bit with your father, don't you? Port to port, traveling the globe, that kind of thing, right?"

Hailey sipped her tea and nodded.

"I'm sure you have tasted quite a bit of treats along the way. The fresh meats from Aibronne, the plentiful fish from Jakar, the exotic spices from Baron's Bay..." He slumped back and sighed dramatically. "Ah, life at sea. Seeing so many places, trying new and different foods." He looked at her directly, and she felt the chill of his gaze. "Reading books from faraway places."

Hailey tried her best not to blush, but she felt color rising in her cheeks. He looked at her for a long moment.

"Yes-s-s," he let the end of the word slide out like the hiss of a snake. "You thought I had forgotten about our conversation at the party about reading. I can see how you would be surprised, especially since I spoke with so many other people that evening."

He paused to sip his tea, then continued.

"But I do love a good story, don't you?" He leaned forward, setting down the cup and looking at her with a predatory grin. "So tell me more about this primer you were reading the other day."

She froze. Her brain screamed at her to say something, anything. Her father's words from the party bubbled up in her mind, and she felt her lips move.

"It belonged to my mother."

"Ah, yes, that's right." He sat back in the chair, picking up a butter knife and looking at it. "Your mother. She died in that horrible incident on Cowl's Ridge, am I right? Dreadful thing." He began to scrape the butter knife across his thumb, looking at it, testing the edge.

"I can see how you are so sentimentally attached to it. Having been your mother's." He shifted in the chair and, while still playing with the knife, looked at her directly. "It's just that, well, the Church has been putting those things out for decades. I've read quite a few different editions and, to be quite honest with you, they are rather" —he made a grasping motion in the air as though he were trying to snatch a word flying in front of him— "dry?" He said the word like a question, as though he weren't fully sure of the word.

He smiled at her and cocked his head as he leaned forward in his chair.

"Now what you have on your hands must be something quite extraordinary. You were so engrossed when I saw you at the market, and the cover looked so elaborately made. I would dearly love to look at this tome." He let his mouth savor the word like a wine, rolling it out dramatically.

"I-I-I don't have it."

"Not with you? A shame." He shifted almost playfully in his chair. "Then again, it would be bad manners to bring a book to a tea party, wouldn't it?"

He snapped his fingers over his head and took a sip of tea. The automaton servant appeared by his side holding a book. *Her* book. The red eyes of the skull stared blankly at her, and she gasped.

As if Graver read her mind, he jumped in.

"Ah! What do we have here? I see that we have your mother's primer after all!"

He took the book from the servant and dismissed him.

"Let's take a look at this."

He turned it over in his hand, admiring the silver and iron works that held it shut.

He scrunched his nose and looked at her. "Kind of odd for a lady's primer, isn't it?" He held up the book to her, pointing out the skull. "I mean the skull is quite unladylike, don't you think?"

Hailey couldn't move. She could only look at the book tumbling in the bishop's hands as he inspected the silver and iron clasps that kept it shut. She wanted it. She needed it back in her hands. She wanted to reach out and grab it from him.

"I do have to say, though, it does look rather interesting. Let's take a look inside, shall we?" Staring intently at her, he handed the book to her, all the while never breaking that toothy smile.

Hailey leapt at it, snatched the book out of his hand, and embraced it. She felt a slight sense of relief to be holding the book. Seeing it in someone else's hands bothered her in some unexplainable way. She looked down at it. She wanted to take it and run, but she knew that there were more than likely guards just outside the doors. If they knew where she hid her book, she was sure that they were watching the house and Grandmother Rose. They were probably watching her father at the guild as well. There were very few places the Crown did not hold sway, and even in those places, the churches heard confessions regularly. No need to spy when people would tell you everything. The book was right. She was in great danger.

Bishop Graver sat patiently expectant. He sat back in his chair and steepled his hands in front of him. He slowly raised an eyebrow at her.

She hated herself for it, but like a good little girl, she did as she was told and touched the skull. The latches sprung open. The bishop sat back up and extended a hand out to her. She reluctantly handed the opened book back to the bishop.

Taking the book, he leaned back in his chair. "Lovely!" He began to leaf through the pages, all of which were still blank. Page after page, the words would not come. He looked up at her.

"So much fuss over a book you cannot read." His face fell in mock disappointment as he sat up promptly and slapped the book shut. "Oh well. The Queen told me I wouldn't be able to read it, anyway."

The comment hung in the air for a long moment. Hailey was stunned.

"She's the one who sent me, you know. She had a feeling that the book would come here and find its way to you."

Recognizing the surprise on her face, he continued.

"Oh, yes, the Veiled Queen knows exactly who you are." He smiled at her and reached for his tea. "Your father, too, and most of those he affiliates with. There aren't many secrets that she isn't privy to, I'm afraid. I was her chief confessor, and even I was amazed to hear the number of secrets that the Veiled Lady knows. No doubt she is watching us even now."

Hailey looked around and saw that the room was still empty save for her and Bishop Graver, who now looked at her coldly over his tea.

"Don't worry. You will see her when the time comes. I'm sure that the two of you will have plenty to discuss."

He shifted in his chair a bit, still keeping his eyes on her.

"It was good of you to accept my invitation. It has been most delightful. I will have to tell your grandmother how exceptionally well behaved you were."

He waved his arm in the air. Behind Hailey, the door creaked open, and she heard the sound of heavy feet approaching behind her. The closer the feet came, the more her heart sank.

"It will provide her with some comfort after we tell her that you and your father have been taken into custody for contraband and conspiracy against the Crown."

She made to get up, but the two guards who stood to each side of her pushed her back down in the chair.

Bishop Graver took a bite of another cookie and poured himself another cup of tea. He placed the cup on the saucer after a long and satisfying sip.

Hailey felt waves of despair washing over her as the large, calloused hands rested on her shoulders. At that moment, she realized how foolish she was. She should have listened to the book. She should have listened to the young man. Even her grandmother was afraid, even though she didn't say it directly. Why had she come? To please her grandmother? To protect her status? Because it was what a young lady was supposed to do? Even she didn't know. All she knew now was that she would be paying the price for her indecision earlier. She should have followed the boy into the crowds and taken her chances.

The bishop addressed the two guards.

"See to it that she is placed on board the *Halifax* right away. The Queen will want her for questioning." He waved again and snapped his fingers at the guards. "See that it's done quietly. No need to raise any attention. We don't want any unrest."

He took the book and handed it to the other guard. "Give this to the boat's captain and be sure that he keeps careful watch on it. The Queen wants that book in her hands as soon as possible. Now off with you."

The towering guards lifted Hailey to her feet, and she tried to utter a scream, but she was instantly muffled by one of the guards holding a rag over her nose and mouth. A pungent scent stifled her scream, and the room began to swirl. She swooned, and the guards hauled her up on her feet and began to drag her along. Just before she passed out completely, the bishop addressed her one last time as she was being dragged from the ballroom.

"Lovely having tea with you, my dear!"

Jacob Graver grinned to himself smugly as he took another sip of tea and reached for another cookie. After placing it in his smiling mouth, he savored it almost as much as he did his victory.

The guards loaded Hailey into the royal carriage and climbed on board. The great steel horses began to pull them down the lane. The great crowds parted as the horses slowly trotted through the crowd of people and down to the docks where the Crown ship, *Halifax,* was waiting to take her to the Queen.

# CHAPTER 12

$I$n the dark of the *Halifax's* hold, all Hailey could do was feel sorry for herself. She had awoken with her hands chained around a post. She didn't know how long she had been unconscious, but it must have been a while because the boat was well under way. Having traveled out of the port with her father so many times, she found it was easy to tell that the boat had made it past the calm cove and the breakwaters and was making its way out to the sea.

Her eyes grew accustomed to the dark, and she saw that the hold of the ship was surprisingly empty—only she and a few crates were on the floor. She sat up as much as she could, the length of chain long enough that she could sit up and even stand, but not much else. Her body ached; she stretched as best as she could, but the chains had little give. On her arm was a sticky patch with a tube that lead to a bag suspended from the top of the pole. She leaned into the post to give her enough room to maneuver her hands around and pull the sticky patch from her forearm. She tossed it and the tube aside. She then stretched and contorted as best she could to check her hair for pins to pick the locks, but they were gone. Her captors had taken them all.

Hailey noticed that there were lights in the hold, the same globe style found in her room, but the crew must have shut them off when they set sail. She thought it must have been done more out of cruelty than to save energy.

She had heard her father talk several times about Crown ships, with their odd, dark, conical sails. Those sails somehow helped produce a limitless magical power that gave them lights, navigation, even communication over long distances. They didn't need large, cumbersome batteries like the devices that merchants had. The sails would pull the energy out of the sky just the same as the wind that billowed the sail.

He would rail for hours on how useful it would be if merchants had access to such things instead of just the Queen's ships. Some of her father's friends had secretly tried to figure out these devices, but they turned out to be far too complicated for them. Even some of the wisest of tinkerers couldn't figure out what they were made of, for nothing like it existed in nature.

Her father! She gasped and began to panic. Bishop Graver had said before she blacked out that he was going to have her father arrested for contraband and conspiracy as well. They were both hanging offenses.

She had no idea how long she had been asleep and on the ship. In the time she was away, her father might have been tried, found guilty, and executed. Was her father still alive?

Large, bitter tears rolled off her cheeks, and she began to sob.

After a while, the tears subsided, and she resigned herself to her situation. There was nothing she could do to save her father, let alone herself. All she could do now was survive as long as she could and see what happened when she went before the Queen.

Above decks, she could hear the shuffle of feet and the voice of the captain booming over the ship, giving instructions for the midday routine. Before the announcements were finished, the lights in the hold began to burn brighter. Hailey's eyes tried to adjust.

She heard the sound of keys rattling in a lock, and in the growing light she could make out a set of stairs just off to her left. A pair of large, ill-fitting boots descended them. The boots belonged to a short, portly, gray-bearded man who was carrying a tray of food. He waddled down the stairs and made his way over to her. He stood and looked at her for a long moment through his round, rimless glasses, as she sat on the floor glowering up at him.

"Ah, such a shame, seein' such a lovely girl so sad." He shook his head. "Touches me heart."

His accent was rough and difficult to understand. He pronounced his words strangely, as though they were foreign to his tongue. It was as if he puzzled over the words as soon as he said them.

"Cap'n said you'd be awake by now, said I should bring yer something ta eat as yer might be hungry. Yer been asleep a good while now. I knows, Cap'n sen' me to check on yer yesterday."

"How long have I been asleep… Mr. uhhh…?" She looked at him, hoping that he would fill in the rest. He looked at her dumbly a moment, then nodded his head as though he got the message.

"Gibson, me name's Gibson, though most folks call me Gibby. We left port three days ago. Yer quite the sound sleeper! Never seen anyone sleep li' tha' before."

Three days. Her father could be long dead by now, and she was three days' sail away.

She felt a new rush of tears begin to well in her eyes, but she bit her lip to stifle them. She had given them enough tears already. Much to her distaste, Gibby noticed.

"Aww, no sense cryin' abou' it. We shouldn't be in port after long." The man placed the tray on her outstretched legs so she could reach it around the post. "Here, have some food. I'm sure yer hungry."

Hailey couldn't even look at the tray.

"Suit yourself. Yer know it gets pretty dark an' lonely down here in the hold. Maybe I should stay down here an' keep yer company."

He sat on the floor by her.

From up the stairs, a voice boomed throughout the ship.

"Gibby, please report to the quarterdeck. Gibby to the quarterdeck."

Gibby sighed and rubbed both hands along his smooth, bald head. "Guess it'll hafta be 'nother time, little missy."

He got up slowly, grunting as he negotiated his way off the floor around his round belly. Once back on his feet, he began to waddle back towards the stairs. Before he went up, he turned back to her and said with a grin, "Bes' eat that. It's not like yer goin' anywhere fer a while."

He proceeded up the stairs and closed the door behind him. The lights dimmed back to the way they were before. Hailey was left to the solitude of the ship's hold and her thoughts.

THE FIRST DAY, she did not touch the food, her guilt and sadness robbing her of her appetite, but the next day she leapt on the food and tore into it with her bare hands the second it was placed on her legs. She leaned into the post and devoured the small cuts of meat and potatoes as though she were a savage animal. After not eating for four days, she was close to eating the tray itself. They were wise to not give her any utensils. Had they, she probably could have used one of them to work the locks around her wrists.

Sometime later—midday, Hailey guessed, from the shuffle on the upper decks—the man known as Gibby came and brought another tray of food, this time with a larger portion. Hailey was glad for this, for the lack of food left her weakened. Food would help her regain at least some of her strength.

Blessedly, his visit was brief, but not brief enough for Hailey's liking. Though the man looked harmless and though he might have possibly been a little slow, there was something dark and craving in his cold look at her. His eyes lingered just a bit too long. It made Hailey uneasy.

The days passed between sleeping, eating, and quiet contemplation. On one of his visits, Gibby had brought her a chamber pot, so she thankfully didn't have to behave like livestock and do her business on the floor.

Gibby was the only person she saw. She sat in the dark hold for hours, days, staring off into the dim light of the cabin and thinking of how she had gotten there. Thinking about the decisions had brought her to be chained in the hold of a ship on her way to stand before the Queen. How she found and took the book. Deciding not to tell her father about it and getting caught up in the mystery of it instead of just getting rid of the stupid thing. She regretted most of all not listening to the book and her instincts. She should have escaped with the boy when she had the chance.

She let her mind play out the possibilities of what would have happened if she had done things differently. Like a good navigator, she plotted out the courses of every outcome, every decision. What if she had never taken the book? The Crown would have had the book and taken her father anyway. But they wouldn't have taken her, would they? She would have been free to try to save her father.

She couldn't get over the way Bishop Graver looked at her. She contemplated it for a long time, trying to figure it out, until it dawned on her what that look meant. Familiarity. He also said that the Queen knew her, knew that the book would come to her. Why would the book come to her? How? If so, did that mean that the Crown would have kidnapped her anyway?

Had she listened to the book or the young man and run, she could have found any of a dozen ships putting out for distant ports that morning. Once under way, she could have gotten word to her father that she was safe and left instructions on how to join her. Her father's merchant guild had contacts everywhere. Any one of them would have been glad to secretly pass along a message, if not hide them altogether. She would have been safe. Her father would have been safe. The book would have been safe, for the time being, at least.

Just thinking about the book made her break out in a cold sweat. She felt the same panic a mother feels when she loses her child in the crowd at the market. Over and over in her head it called out to her, and Hailey could not go to it. Its cries went unanswered.

None of this would have happened if she had listened to the book and the young man. So why didn't she do it? Why did she freeze in place when she should have been running away?

The answer came in the voice of her grandmother clucking in her head. Over and over, she heard Rose tell her about the duties and the responsibilities of being a lady. How she was expected to serve and submit, both to their elders and to men of stature and status. Her grandmother, in sync with the teachings of the Church and their schools and primers, helped hammer in the virtues that forged the chains that bound her now. Rather than defying those virtues and being her own woman, she'd submitted to the things that she did not like or understand to make her grandmother happy.

She had seen so much sorrow in her family when her mother died, especially in her father. She recalled how he would sit for hours at a time, silent and still, as if waiting for death. It had driven her to constantly try to make him and everyone around her happy. Now she hated that incessant need to please others.

Hailey also thought about the state of the world. It had not always been like this, no matter how hard the Crown and the Church tried to wipe away the record. She had read the histories of it from long before she was born. Men and women were equal and free, even the redheads, once. There was a republic and a senate, where men and women had an equal voice in the world in which they lived. That had ended when the first king seized control some 250 years ago. And with each passing year and each passing monarch since, the Crown's grip grew tighter and tighter.

There was a rebellion by the colonies some 50 years after the Crown had been established. The rebels fought to restore everyone's freedoms and abolish the Crown, but failed. Determined to avoid another insurrection by the common folk, the Crown formed an alliance with the Church of the Ancestors to ensure that both remained in power, uncontested.

They designed a system that created a constant thirst for wealth and position that the Church wove through the very fabric of their society. The Church ran everything that the Queen did not. They printed the books, they ran the schools, and they ran the spiritual lives of everyone. The Queen might control their bodies and wealth, but the Church owned their hearts and minds.

One of the core beliefs the Church taught was that a

lady's place was to be a servant to men and her elders. They preached salvation through status and wealth. It was the litany of a system that supported the Crown—mind, body, and soul, all born in the time of the first Ancestors who fell from the sky.

Hailey thought of the book and one important thing it had told her: She wasn't alone. There was a pirate queen once, a captain on the high seas who defied the Crown and was their scourge. She made a difference. That book was proof of it. Even though she didn't have the book with her, she had the knowledge of its existence. It was a small treasure within herself telling her that her heart wasn't wrong. She could be something other than a wife. She could be the captain she always wanted to be someday if, like the Pirate Queen Rachel, she fought for it.

Hailey shifted and felt the shackles on her wrists pinch. Oddly the rattle of the chains brought back a memory she had forgotten. On one of their trade runs, her father was carrying a load of cattle in the hold of his ship. Hailey was fascinated with them. She had never been up close to cattle before. They never put up a fuss and went wherever they were led. She remembered how complacent those cows were, how calm.

Sitting there reflecting on it in the dark, Hailey found herself wondering if they knew they were being shipped to their slaughter. Until now, she'd never stopped to wonder if they cared.

They had been shackled to a pole just as she was.

THE DAYS WENT BY SLOWLY, only punctuated by the brief visits and leering looks of Gibby. He only came to feed her once a day, so it was easy to track the time, though difficult to keep up her energy.

On the tenth day, something seemed different about Gibby. He raised the light level a bit more than usual, and he was much more conversational and more careless. He left the door open at the top of the stairs. As he placed the tray on the floor by Hailey, she could smell the tart smell of cheap wine on him.

"I get ta go off duty soon. For a few 'ole days! Want ta celebrate wit me?"

He slumped to the floor and pulled out a small flagon of wine, showing it to her. She looked around the room. Though it looked brighter, the room suddenly felt colder.

He took a swig and offered it to her, but she shook her head.

"Right. Too good ta 'ave a drink wit' a common man, are ya?"

The words came out mumbled and marked with more of a heavier accent than usual.

"Fine time ta take some leave. Yer think the cap'n would at least give me a good night ta be off. Fog so thick up ther yer can' hardly see yer hand in front o' yer face."

The cold bite of a chill sank onto the back of Hailey's neck as she remembered what the book had told her. She looked up the stairs, eyes wide.

"The mists?" she murmured.

He looked at her and started laughing. "Yer afraid o' the fog, love? Scared the mean, nasty pirates goin' ta get yer? Well, don' worry, love. They ain't real." He leaned back and propped himself up on one arm. "I been on these seas since I was a lad and I can tell yer now, ther' ain't no such thing." He leaned forward and patted her knee.

Hailey looked up the stairs again, and this time she noticed that the mists he spoke of had started to slowly descend the stairs. She turned back to him and noticed that he had slid a little closer to her. Too close.

"Yer know, we 'ave a couple o' days ta get ta know each other…"

He reached over and stroked the side of her cheek. Something inside of her screamed out. She wasn't sure if it was the voice of her mother or herself way down inside, but she knew one thing: She had to fight.

"No!" She jerked her head away and kicked out with her feet, kicking him firmly on his soft round belly and sending him backwards. There was a commotion upstairs and the sound of hurried feet on the decks above. Gibby paid it no mind as his face darkened, and he howled obscenities at Hailey while cradling his belly. Hailey stood up.

She was malnourished and weak, but she wasn't going to go down without a fight. She was worth fighting for. She felt a volcano swell up in her full of rage about her life, her situation, and her mother's death. She hated those who had put her there, who took her mother away from her, and now her father. A scream escaped her as she lunged at the charging oaf.

Her hands were bound too close to the pole for her to be able to punch him, but her legs were free. She caught him again with her heel, this time in his chest. Gibby let out a whoosh of air and began to go down, grabbing her ankle as he fell. They both crashed to the deck, and he began to climb closer to her, using her leg like a rope on the rigging. She screamed again, trying to push him off of her, but her strength was beginning to fail. He was close to her face now, and she could smell the sweat and sour wine on his breath, as he shouted at her to be still.

He punched her in the head, and her vision swam. He tried to push his whole weight on her to pin her down, but she kept fighting, trying to twist away. She had just enough room to be able to land some blows with her fist on his head and neck, but the chains slowed her punches, and they bounced off of him. She bit him hard on the cheek, hard enough to draw blood. The man cried out and rolled off of her. Gibby stood over her, screaming more obscenities at her while holding his bloody cheek.

She looked up at him defiantly, and spit at him. Hailey tried to catch her breath and steel herself for another attack. She was tiring quickly, but she had enough in her for one more round.

Gibby waited too long, and Hailey quickly sent a shoeless foot to his crotch, doubling him over.

He lay on the ground cursing at her and spitting. She wouldn't be so lucky next time. Hailey watched as Gibby slowly pulled himself from the deck and produced a dagger.

Hailey's eyes went wide and stayed transfixed on the blade.

"Cap'n says we 'ave to ta' yer to the Queen. 'e didn' say in one piece."

He was only a few paces away. Hailey steeled herself for the attack, but it never came. He simply stopped mid-stride and stood there staring at her. Then from his chest, a bloom of blood spread across his dingy white shirt. He looked down at it in surprise and then fell to the ground, dead.

Behind his body stood two figures with bright glowing eyes. The tallest one held a black blade, wet with the blood of her assailant. Its large captain's hat rested like a crown on its nest of hair, and the still face of the skull stared at her. In the figure's other hand she could see the book, *her* book, its bright red eyes beckoning to her with the same glow as the pirate's eyes.

At its side stood another figure, though not as tall and well developed as the giant captain. It pointed at her and said to the ghost captain.

*"The Navigator."*

The pirate captain nodded and turned to the other figure and spoke.

*"Bring her. Sink the ship."*

It sheathed its blade, turned, and disappeared up the stairs. The other figure advanced on Hailey. She was too tired to fight. She didn't know if it was the blow to her head, the lack of food, or the whole ordeal, but she felt woozy and knew she couldn't get up. The mists had fully engulfed the room. The ghost pirate advanced on her, red eyes blazing through the mists. She lost consciousness just before the figure touched her.

# CHAPTER 13

$\mathcal{H}$ailey awoke, gasping and flailing her arms. She bolted upright in the bed, looking around frantically. "Help!" she cried.

"Whoa, whoa, whoa, relax! It's just a side effect of the gas."

Her head seemed fuzzy, and the room was too bright, but the voice was deep and oddly soothing.

"Where are the pirates?" She looked about the room frantically, expecting to see the glowing eyes staring at her. Instead there was only a single figure sitting beside her. She stopped and focused on him. It was the young man from the village with the odd eyes.

Hailey sat in stunned silence for a moment, then looked down at herself and let out a gasp. Her dress was gone; instead, she was wearing someone else's long shirt.

She looked at him wildly. "Where are my clothes?"

"Hold on!" He put his hands out in front of him, open palmed and waving. "You were a mess when we found you."

He got up from the stool and headed to the back of the cabin by the windows. Looking at them, she noticed that they were obscured by mists.

"So you're in the habit of stealing clothes as well as kidnapping people?" Hailey pulled the covers up to her chin and balled up her hands, eyes tracking the boy as he paced.

He looked over at her and chuckled. She sat and eyed him back.

"No, not regularly, we just think that those we kidnap shouldn't smell." He grinned at her, and she blushed. She didn't have a comeback for that. Her head was still cloudy.

He resumed his pacing and looked out the window as if waiting for something. Hailey thought to break the awkward silence that had grown in the cabin.

"I thought you were skeletons or ghosts or something. You look pretty real to me."

"Well, I am real enough. What you saw, those skull faces, were the masks. We call them rebreathers. They let us see through the mists, breathe, and communicate with each other. The mists we generate have a mixture in them that makes you sleepy and stupid. The masks protect us from the effects and help to scare everyone who isn't wearing one. It makes raids easier."

He poured a glass of water from the crystal pitcher on the captain's table and brought it, a large apple, and a large hunk of bread to her. He paced back across the room from her, thankfully keeping his back to her as she devoured the food.

"So where are we?" She pulled off the covers and moved towards the edge of the bed. Her wrists were still sore from having been in manacles so long, and she was bruised and battered but thankfully alive. She sat on the end of the bed, careful to be sure the shirt did not ride up and reveal too much.

"You're on our ship, the *Dark Star*. The captain had us put you in his quarters until you woke up."

She looked about the cabin. It was larger than her father's, but its layout was nearly the same. This cabin seemed warmer to her, much more lived in. She tried to put a finger on why she thought that, but it eluded her.

She tried to get up but found her legs unstable. The boy was at her side instantly and caught her. His speed made her gasp in surprise.

"Whoa there. Try not to move too fast. The stuff in the gas is still in your system. It should wear off soon, but try not to move too fast until then."

He held her for a long moment. Suddenly it struck Hailey that she was in a cabin alone with a handsome young man. Her face quickly went hot, and she looked away from his arresting pale brown eyes.

From across the cabin, the door burst open and light footsteps closed on them.

"Hadyn!" a female voice cried. "I leave for just a couple of minutes, and you're already putting the moves on her?"

The young man, Hadyn, turned and gave the speaker an embarrassed look.

"Hey now, Kyra, it's not what it looks like." Hadyn released Hailey, who sank back into the bed.

The dark-skinned girl advanced on them. Her red hair was long and curly and held back in a red bandana. Her deck shorts and striped shirt looked as if they were a hundred years old. From her thick belt hung two long knives, one on each side. She was shorter than Hadyn, but not by much.

"Oh, really?" She smiled at Hailey, then looked back to him and placed her hands on her hips.

"Yeah, she was just trying to get up, and she lost her balance." He stepped back from Hailey and scratched the back of his head.

Kyra noticed Hailey was trying to pull down the shirt more to cover up. The shirt went down to her thighs, and Kyra knew Hailey didn't have anything else underneath since she was the one who had bathed and dressed Hailey earlier.

"Well, why don't you be a gentleman and see if you can find her some pants before she catches a cold," Kyra said to him, cocking her head.

There was an awkward pause, then Hadyn looked at Kyra.

"I was just about to go do that." His answer seemed to be more sarcastic than informative. He looked back at Hailey. "I'll be right back." With that, he left the cabin.

Kyra stood smiling at Hailey, one hand on her hip.

"Don't mind lover boy over there. He's a pretty one, but sometimes not too bright. He's harmless for the most part."

Hailey looked embarrassed and tried to hide her blush. She thought him attractive, something she had never really experienced before.

Kyra slowly closed the distance and sat down beside her on the bed, careful to adjust the long blades on her belt.

Not wanting to be rude, Hailey tried to introduce herself, but Kyra beat her to it.

"Hailey Heartstone, right?" Kyra said, pointing at her and smiling. Surprised, Hailey could only mutely nod at her.

"My name is Kyra, Kyra Faber. Pleased to meet you!" Kyra leaned towards her. "So you are the famous Navigator every-one's been talking about."

"How do you know?"

"We've been watching you for a while." Kyra's grin was almost mischievous. "Once we figured out who you were and that you had the book, we tried to reach you."

"Hadyn."

Kyra nodded her head.

"Why didn't you go with him?" Kyra looked at her, cocking her head.

"Well, I don't know. I guess I was kinda scared by the whole thing." Hailey shrugged.

"Understandable. Hadyn is cute, but he isn't the best conversationalist." Kyra chuckled to herself.

The door reopened, and Hadyn came striding in, a pair of long shorts in his hand. "Here you go." He tossed Hailey the pants, and she eagerly began to slip them on.

Kyra shot Hadyn a look that told him that he should look the other way. Hadyn shrugged and turned around, looking out the windows at the back of the cabin.

Hailey stood up slowly, holding on to Kyra's shoulder. She could stand, but just barely. Her leg strength had only slightly returned to her, and she felt off balance and weak. Her stomach growled in protest and demanded it be filled.

Standing there, she noted something odd. They told her she was on a ship, but she didn't feel the customary sway a ship had, even when anchored. As she worked on putting on the shorts, she wondered if this was a side effect of the gas.

Hadyn spoke to them over his shoulder.

"Captain said to show her around the ship and get her something to eat. He'll meet with her back here later." He must have heard her stomach's loud roar.

"Great!" Kyra grabbed Hailey's arm and pulled her past Hadyn. "Let's go get you something to eat! I'll show you around on the way."

Hailey saw that on Kyra's right hand she had a woven ring with the skull. Its red eyes seemed to glint at her as the wearer pulled her along. Hailey's legs were not completely steady yet, and she stumbled to keep up.

"Hey, wait a minute!" Hadyn exclaimed, but by the time he could lodge his protest, they were already out the cabin door.

Once outside the cabin, Hailey froze in her tracks. It wasn't the crew that disturbed her; they looked normal enough. It wasn't the dark sails or the thick mists that looked almost as if the ship was sailing on them. It was the fact that over the rails, just above the mists, she could see that they were several hundred feet up in the air. The air felt cool as it brushed her cheeks, and it stung her lungs slightly with the chill of it. The air seemed almost thinner, light, and without the tart salt smell, as she was used to. It was unbelievably refreshing.

She went to the side rail and looked at the whole of the ocean that stretched out before her. Dawn had just broken, just as when she had been standing watch on her father's mast a few weeks prior. This time the view was much more commanding. On the port horizon, a long land mass poked out of the blue waters.

Kyra joined her and noted the shocked expression on Hailey's face. Kyra smiled.

"Hadyn didn't tell you we were in the air?"

Hailey's face was pale. Quietly, slowly, the words rolled out of her mouth.

"He said we were on a ship."

Kyra chuckled, embraced Hailey's shoulders, and looked her in the eyes. "It's a ship of the air, actually. Look up." Kyra extended one long finger, pointing up, and both of them raised their gaze. Past the black rigging and sail of the ship, they could see a pair of long, dark balloons the ship was tethered to.

"What magic is this?" Hailey wondered out loud.

"No magic, dear. Just science. Leftovers handed down from the days of the original Pirate Queen. Most of the crew are descendants of her original shipmates. I'll tell you about it later. Come on, I'll show you around."

They passed several deckhands, most of whom looked like skeletons in clothes, but upon closer inspection they were nothing more than automatons similar to the ones she had seen in the colonial mansion. They had the same dead eyes.

Each automaton diligently worked on one of the tasks keeping the ship going. It made sense to Hailey, in an ironic sort of way. Hailey noted that there weren't many humans about on the ship, so it would make sense to have the automatons take up the slack. In a way, they really were a skeleton crew. Hailey snickered at the idea.

The figures ignored Hailey and Kyra as the two young women passed but focused only on their work. Hailey made sure to give them a wide berth. Their eyes still unnerved her.

Reaching the bow of the ship, Kyra leaned over the rail and pointed out two vents on each side. Thick volumes of mist poured out from each side and obscured them from view below.

"From below we just look like a cloud." Kyra grinned at her. They both stood up straight. "Pretty clever, huh?"

"Yeah." Hailey looked back over the deck of the ship. Everything looked relatively normal, with the exception of the dark wooden hull and the black sails. On each side of the stern, she could see something sticking up. She pointed at them and asked, "What's that?"

"Fins. Like a fish. They help us to steer when we are in the air. Come on, I'll show you!"

The ship wasn't quite as long as the *Arrow*, nor was it as towering as the *Vigilant*, but everything she saw about her said that this was a very capable and maneuverable warship, albeit a bit dated.

Over the rear side rail, they took a closer look at two long planks that ran out from either side, the ends capped with long kite-like shapes. While looking down at them, Hailey could see the occasional breaks of blue snaking through the carpet of mists they rode.

"So what's the masks, the mists, and the flying for?" Hailey tried to not sound incredulous, but after all she had been through, it was just too hard to believe anything.

"That's easy. Freedom. As I said, most of the crew are descendants of the first pirate crew, but not all of them. Take me for example." She held out a curl of long red hair to show her. "I was once a slave."

"You mean a servant?" Hailey thought of the servants around her father's house. All of them had the same red hair, and now that she thought of it, the same haunted look.

"No. A slave." She was curt with her response and folded her arms, shifting her posture and jutting out her hip. She continued.

"Most redheads come from the northern regions of the mainland of Phesin. We try our best to hide, but the Crown regularly hunts us down and rounds us up for labor. The lucky ones get sold to the colonies as servants, the unlucky ones are bound for the mines in Vregora. I was one of the unlucky ones."

Hailey stood there, horrified. She had no idea that redheads were actually enslaved. She always thought that they were hired hands and liked their work; that was what they taught in the Church-run schools.

As if reading her face, Kyra stepped to her and put a friendly hand on her shoulder. "It's okay. You probably didn't know. Most people don't."

Hailey remembered learning in school about the only people in the world who looked different from everyone else. Other than differences between the sexes, there wasn't much else different from one person to another save a slight variation of how brown your skin was or the occasional blonde streaks in your brown hair, like Hailey's. Anything different was considered abnormal and inferior bordering on freakish.

In the Church schools, teachers taught that those with red hair were not just physically different from everyone else. They were not as developed or refined as everyone else. They were certainly less intelligent than everyone, but they had a saving grace—they were incredibly hard workers. The Church and the Crown believed that giving those with red hair menial work was a blessing to them. It gave their lives a place and a purpose. It was the will of the Ancestors that these rare people serve normal people, and they were happy to do so. Why else would the Ancestors have marked them so? No one ever said anything about slavery.

Kyra continued, her voice now lowered with an edge of bitterness. "I was young when it happened. My family and I were caught and thrown into the hold of a ship bound for Vregora. Luckily, we ran into a squall that dashed us against the rocks off the coast. Not many of us survived—my family didn't. Those who were still alive clung to the rocks for all their worth as the sea boiled around us. One by one, people slipped off the rocks and into the cruel waters. Not me." She grinned at Hailey. "I was the last one left. I was just about to let go when out of the clouds floats this ship. They rescued me, brought me aboard, broke my chains, and I've been a crewman ever since."

Hailey stood there, stunned. She searched for the right words to say, but couldn't find them. Her body fortunately decided to break the awkward silence. Hailey's stomach began to growl loudly again. Kyra looked down at Hailey's stomach in surprise and then up at her.

"I think it's time we get you something to eat," she said, laughing.

On their way down below decks, Kyra showed her the gun batteries, several lines of cannons all nestled home in their berths, waiting for the moment to spring out from behind their outward covers. There were more cannons than Hailey expected, thirty-six in all, and a full gun crew of people who sat idly by playing cards. They didn't pay Hailey or Kyra a moment's regard, as the girls passed by and headed down to the galley.

Kyra motioned for Hailey to sit down at one of the long empty benches and disappeared into the kitchen.

Hailey looked around. She was impressed with how neat and tidy their galley was. Kyra emerged from the kitchen with two large steaming bowls and placed one in front of Hailey.

Hailey delighted in the smell of the beef stew set before her. It was something she hadn't had for a long time, beef being so rare now. As hungry as she was, she could have eaten a whole cow, given the chance.

"There you go. There's plenty more where that came from, so eat up." Kyra sat down across from her. Hailey began to wolf down the stew.

If her grandmother had seen how Hailey attacked her bowl, she would have been horrified and called her a wild animal. Hailey didn't care; she shoveled in the food as fast as she could. Once the bowl was empty, Kyra took it and refilled it for her, which Hailey promptly finished as well. After her second bowl, she started to slow down and regained some small resemblance of humanity.

"So," Hailey said, looking up at Kyra and speaking around a mouthful of stew, "your crew found out I had been taken and what, followed me?"

Her grandmother would have been appalled at her speaking with her mouth full. She didn't care one bit.

"Something like that. It took a while for Hadyn to get back to us and tell us what was going on. I hear we got there just in time." Kyra looked at her with an eyebrow raised.

Hailey paused in eating, lost in thought about her fighting off the drunken Gibby. She had never been more terrified in all of her life, but she had survived it with her dignity intact. She shuddered, grunted an affirmative, and went back to eating.

The combination of the food and the gas wearing off sparked her thoughts. She thought back to how she got there. Her meeting with Bishop Graver and then being taken away…. She dropped her spoon, and her eyes flew wide open. She bolted upright.

"Dad!" Hailey blurted.

Kyra looked at her, surprised.

"The bishop said he was going to arrest my dad. We have to save him." She stood up and looked imploringly at Kyra.

Kyra reached across the table and took her hand. "Relax. Last we heard he wasn't in jail. Even if he was, he won't be going anywhere anytime soon."

Hailey sat back down with an exasperated sigh. "What does that mean?"

"Don't worry, we have eyes and ears everywhere." She pointed her spoon at Hailey. "We found you, right?"

Hailey looked down into her half-eaten bowl of stew and pushed around some carrots. She had lost her appetite.

"We will find out from the captain during the meeting." Kyra grinned at her.

"Meeting?" Hailey looked up at her.

"The senior staff meeting." Hadyn's deep, smooth, confident voice preceded him as he strode quickly into the galley. "Captain's sent me to come get you."

Kyra turned and looked up at him.

"Excellent timing, Mr. Winder! We were just finishing. Be a dear and clean up after us, will you?" Kyra said with a mischievous twinkle in her eye.

"Clean u— Kyra!" protested Hadyn.

Turning back to Hailey, Kyra took her by the hand and stood up.

"Let's go talk to the captain."

They both stood up, and Kyra began to lead her out quickly before Hadyn could protest further. He grumbled to himself and began to collect their bowls.

Kyra and Hailey made their way back up the stairs and out of the hold and emerged onto the deck. Only the skeleton crew remained, mechanically taking care of the ship in flight. Kyra pulled Hailey past them and across the deck to the cabin.

Now Hailey hoped she would find out how they knew her father was still alive.

# CHAPTER 14

The door opened, and Hailey immediately felt the eyes of the room's occupants upon her as she followed Kyra in. The already small cabin was made even smaller by the press of people. Hailey counted six other people in the room, two sitting, the rest standing.

She recognized the captain behind the desk; he was dressed the same as before, but his dark face was much different from the skull and piercing red eyes he had worn earlier. His face was rough with a scraggly beard speckled with white hair. While his eyes weren't the glowing red of the mask, something in them was just as fierce. Hailey tried not to flinch or look away as he appraised her.

Kyra motioned for her to take one of the two chairs across from the captain, the other already occupied with a bespectacled gentleman, his eyes obscured by the reflection of light in his glasses. He watched her with amused curiosity as she sat.

"So. You are the Navigator," the captain's deep voice rolled out. Hailey looked around the room to the mix of impassive and curious faces. There was a long silence. She wondered if they were waiting for her to tell them something.

The captain burst into motion and bolted forward, startling Hailey. She thought he was going to reach across and grab her, but instead in one swift, smooth motion, he opened a drawer and tossed a book on the desk. It was her book. The Book of the Navigator. The sound of its hitting the table was like a thunderclap that made Hailey jump.

"Prove it," he rumbled and sat back in his chair.

The ruby eyes of the book patiently looked up at her from the table. She wanted to snatch up the book, run with it, and keep running, but just looking at the towering hulk of a man to the captain's right told her she wouldn't get far without being stopped, or worse.

Besides, were she to escape the cabin, where could she go? She didn't have wings, and a fall from that height would break her neck as soon as she hit the water. Once again she was trapped.

She felt the eyes of everyone in the room upon her, watching, waiting expectantly. She was dealing with seagoing people. Granted, they also flew in an airship, but they were seagoing nonetheless. That meant she had room for negotiation. If she wanted them to save her father, she would have to prove that she had something to offer.

Rather than pick up the book, she closed her eyes and felt for it both with her hands and her mind. That itching in her brain increased, and she could almost hear the book whispering to her. She extended her hand over it, and the latches fell away without her touch. She heard creaking, as if everyone around the table had leaned in to get a look.

She opened her eyes and reached over and opened the cover, revealing the first page, then sat back in her chair. The page she turned to was blank. They all looked at each other, confused, then turned to Hailey. She simply smiled and pointed back to the page. They all let their gaze follow her finger, and slowly bubbling up on the surface of the page, letters formed that all could see.

> *TO REACH THE TREASURE,*
> *YOU MUST LISTEN TO THIS GIRL,*
> *MY BLOOD HEIR, HAILEY HEARTSTONE.*
> *SHE WILL LEAD YOU THERE.*
> *SHE IS TO BE YOUR NAVIGATOR.*

A signature sprawled underneath the words in long looping letters, spelling out a name.

*Rachel Feron*

The Pirate Queen herself.

The smudge-covered young woman to Hailey's right broke the silence first. "Wow," she said as she leaned back and buried her hands in her large baggy pants. Beside her, a tall, rakish man with a thin, well-trimmed mustache whistled a descending note and looked at the smudge-covered girl. The others grunted their acknowledgment of what they had seen.

Hailey heard Hadyn's voice from behind her. She hadn't noticed him come in.

"I told you." She didn't even have to turn around to know that he was smirking at the lot of them.

"It seems that we are in good company, then!" said the captain. "Let me introduce myself. I am Telos Zordebran, the elected captain of the *Dark Star*."

He motioned to the large, burly, bald man with the long mustache behind him to his right. "This is Olau Lucki, my first mate."

The large man was shirtless save for a leather vest, under which there was a large tattoo of a skull across his chest. He nodded his head to her and raised his left arm in greeting. At the end of the arm, where a hand should be, was a long, curved hook that glinted wickedly in the light of the room.

The captain motioned to Olau's right, where a short, stocky man stood hunched over; his face, wild dark hair, and beard were covered in soot. "Gunner Malik Smit." Hailey had seen him earlier on the way to the galley. He had a wild look in his eye and smiled a little too broadly for any sane man. Then again, being trapped below decks running the cannon crews on a flying pirate ship would test the limits of any man's sanity.

The captain motioned to the man in the chair. "This is our ship's surgeon, Ciro Vinkler." The man tipped his tall hat at her and offered a small sterile smile to her.

"To your right are Chloe Winsor, our engineer." She looked at the smudge-covered girl and then to the tall man with the pencil-thin mustache to her right. "And the sailing master, Dan Ellis." Chloe gave a friendly wave, and Dan did a simple nod of his head.

"You've already met our second and third mates, Hadyn and Kyra." Hailey nodded her head.

"Good," he said, leaning back in his chair and smiling. "Now we can get down to business. I guess I should welcome you to the crew." The captain's deep and lightly accented voice seemed a bit warmer to her this time, but only slightly. He sat forward in his chair.

"Wait a minute." Hailey's heart began to beat quickly. She knew that she had some leverage now. They wanted her on their crew. They wanted to find the treasure. She held the upper hand here; she just had to have the guts to prove it.

Hailey sat forward in her chair, looking as though she were about to jump out of it.

"What about my dad? Is he still alive?"

"Last report says so," said the captain as he leaned back into his chair.

"Then we have to go get him!"

Telos and Hailey stared at one another for a long, tense moment, neither of them flinching. Hailey remembered a phrase that had been repeated to her over and over again throughout her life. A simple rule in a life at sea: The captain's hand is on the wheel, but it is the navigator who tells him where to go.

The surgeon, Ciro, broke the silence by gently offering, "We wouldn't be able to even if we tried."

Hailey looked at him and sat back in her chair to take the man in.

"What do you mean?"

"There are reports that after you were taken, your father found out and started an uprising."

Hailey felt herself tearing up, but bit her lip. She was negotiating with pirates here. She couldn't afford to show weakness. The doctor continued calmly, as if delivering a report.

"They forced the bishop and his staff to flee the island. In response, the Crown has moved in and blockaded the port. We barely got our informants out in time. I'm afraid that no one is getting in or out of Daden for the time being."

Hailey looked incredulously at Zordebran.

"You have a flying ship!"

"And they have an armada," the captain replied.

Hadyn stepped forward and placed his hand on her shoulder. It was warm, and his grip was soft, comforting.

"If you want to save your father, we need to get to the treasure. Quickly."

Hailey saw that the captain and first officer both shot Hadyn a glance. What was going on? Why did they need to get to the treasure in order to save her father? Hailey's mind raced to figure it out, but was stumped.

She looked up at Hadyn. "Why do we need to find the treasure first, and what's the hurry?"

Hadyn nodded to the surgeon. Hailey turned and looked at Ciro as he removed his glasses and began to clean them with a handkerchief. He spoke, not looking at her.

"Our most recent reports tell us that the Queen ordered Daden to be cleansed, I'm afraid. It looks as though she put the plan in motion a few weeks ago when the book first appeared."

Hailey looked at him, puzzled. "What does that mean?"

Kyra took a step forward and stood in between Hailey and Ciro.

"It means she's planning to wipe them out."

Hailey's jaw dropped open as Kyra continued. "The Queen has a weapon, a man-made plague, that she uses to keep everyone in line. If a town or province acts up, she blockades them and releases it to wipe everyone out. After everyone is gone, she recolonizes the area with new settlers."

Hailey felt numb, and the words fell out of her mouth like cannon balls plunging into the deep. "Cowl's Ridge."

It was Cowl's Ridge all over again.

The ridge had been a hotbed of insurrectionists with many factions, each with the goal to undermine the Queen's rule. It was considered to be a poor area with little resources. Hailey's mother, Rebecca, was there visiting, taking care of a pregnant friend in the last stages of pregnancy. Hailey and her father were set to get them out of there a few days later. When Hailey and her father arrived at the edge of the town, the military had set up a quarantine. The soldiers said that some kind of plague had broken out, and no one was allowed in or out. The plague killed everyone who was trapped there in the quarantine, including her mother. Hailey and her father weren't even allowed to claim her body.

Now Hailey realized that Cowl's Ridge wasn't an accident, or chance, or the will of the Ancestors as the priests told her. It was genocide, and for all she knew, the priests knew, too.

Hailey's hands clawed at the arms of the chair and her face felt hot with rage. She struggled to speak.

"So what does the murdering of all those people have to do with the treasure?"

The engineer, Chloe, stepped forward and stooped down to get eye level with her and placed a hand on Hailey's knee, trying to comfort her.

"The plague is another tool, just like these lights." She pointed to the glowing light on the desk. "The blimp, the mists, the masks, even your book. They are all tools and treasures left behind by our ancestors. The largest collection of those treasures are in a secret cave that only your book can leads us to. One of the treasures in the cave turns the plague on and off. Right now they can't control the plague, all they can do is set it off and wait till everyone dies. If they get their hands on that controller before we do..."

Malik, the gunner, jumped in. "The plague goes from being a cannonball to a time bomb that they can set off at any time."

Hailey tried to talk, but her breaths were coming out too quick and sharp. Time bombs? Cannonballs? She felt as though there were a cannonball resting on her chest.

"H-h-how do you know?" She struggled to get the words out, fighting off the tears that wanted to come.

"History," the sailing master volunteered. "During the War for Independence a couple of hundred years ago or so, your ancestor, Rachel Feron, the first Pirate Queen, led a band of privateers on the ship, the *Revenge*, against the Crown. They almost turned the tide of the war, actually." He stood and strode to the window and looked out. "At one point, the Crown tried to use the plague to wipe out another town. That time it was Rachel's hometown of Jakar. Rachel and her crew were able to stop the plague just in time with something she kept in the treasure cave."

"How do we know we aren't too late already?"

"We don't know much about the plague, but we think it takes time to work," the surgeon said. "I suspect there might be an incubation period of some sort. We think it might take several weeks before any symptoms appear. Then it comes on quite suddenly. The patient starts bleeding from the nose, followed by bleeding from the eyes and ears..." His voice trailed off as he saw the gravity of the room go from low to subterranean.

"I think that's enough, Doctor," the captain gently suggested.

*Several weeks?* Hailey thought. *Could that mean I have the virus, too?* Hailey felt a deep pit forming in her stomach at the thought. Though she had never seen any of the bodies from Cowl's Ridge, by all accounts the results were horrifying. Reports of their gruesome and painful deaths were well known.

"So we have time?" Hailey looked at him.

"If we get to that device Rachel used, then yes," he replied.

Hailey didn't have a choice anymore. She had to save her family. These people were willing to help her get what could save them all. There was nothing more she could negotiate. She wasn't sure she could trust them, but they had saved her from the Crown before. It was obvious that she was too important to betray, at least for the moment.

Hailey turned to the captain.

"What do I need to do?"

Zordebran slid the book to her on the table.

"Be our navigator. Consult your book, see what it says. Find out where we need to go and plot our course."

She picked it up and nodded. Standing, she walked past Hadyn and Kyra, who both gave her sympathetic looks, and went and sat on the bed at the back of the cabin.

The other crewmen continued the meeting, each executive officer giving their reports on their sections. Hailey ignored them and let herself get lost in the book. She looked up at the living map spread out before her in the air. She could see a great many things, but there was nothing about a treasure on it. She looked at her home port of Daden. Dozens of warships blockaded the port. Hailey wondered just how long her father, Grandmother Rose, and the other townsfolk could hold out.

She needed answers. She looked down at the blank page that stared up at her and projected her thoughts to the book.

*Where is the treasure?*

Words bubbled up on the page.

***GOOD! YOU ARE GETTING THE HANG OF THIS!***
***THE TREASURE CAVE IS HIDDEN, EVEN FROM ME.***
***TO FIND OUT ITS LOCATION, YOU MUST FIRST GET***
***THE KEY***
***FROM THE PIRATE QUEEN'S COVE***
***THAT KEY WILL UNLOCK THE LOCATION OF THE***
***TREASURE ON THE MAP,***
***AND THEN I CAN TELL YOU WHERE IT IS.***

*Okay, so where's the cove?*

## *THE PIRATE QUEEN CAN TELL YOU...*

The page went blank for a moment, then a different sort of writing began to fill the page. Hailey flipped the pages and saw that all the once-blank pages were covered in writing. It wasn't block text, as when the book talked to her. This was different. It was actual handwriting. The looping fashion of the words on the page made Hailey think of someone using a quill. Most of the words on the page were blurred except for certain sections. It took her a moment to figure out that the book was showing her just the sections in relation to her question.

*7, Octurine 5546*

*I think I have located a safe harbor on the island of Eolan. It is tricky to get to, but that may be to our advantage. Since accepting the colonial alliance's letter of mark eight months ago, we have either captured or raided a dozen ships and helped to lay siege to the key port in Aibronne. We have been nuisance enough now that they are actively hunting us. Only our good luck and this book have helped us in avoiding the several 80-gun warships they send looking for us. It seems our efforts have given them somewhat of a black eye. They have taken to calling me the Queen of the Pirates and are now offering a large sum of gold for my head. It would be a good idea to find a port of our own than tempt anyone at the colonial ports. They are having a hard enough time as it is keeping people fed and fighting; no need to give them the temptation of a king's ransom to betray one of their own.*

*Though the crown pursues us, they have yet to catch sight of us unless we want them to. With our smaller, more agile ship, and the aid of this journal, we have made a mockery of their hunt, but still, we need a place to rest and refresh our supplies.*

The rest of the sections were blurred, and a colored

arrow pointed to the edge of the page. Hailey guessed that meant she should turn the page.

>*30, Octurine 5546*
>
>*We have established a harbor just off the lip of Eolan. After several days of digging narrow channels up the river to accommodate the Revenge, we reached a spot where we could carve out a small port that is completely hidden from view. I will put the coordinates for it in the notes.*

Again there was nothing left for her to read on the page. Arrows pointed on page after page of blurred texts. Finally, towards the end of the book, a small section remained unblurred.

>*12, Tredecim 5550*
>
>*Things do not bode well. With the recent losses in Baron's Bay, the colonial alliance is on the verge of collapse. We are making our last stop in the cove to hide the key to the treasure cave we have found. I had hoped to go back there and get some of the magical items in the cave to help, but there is no time. We have to get to McKinnett before it's too late. Damn Elias's treachery!*
>
>*I plan to send this book to a separate location for safekeeping after we leave the cove. We just can't afford to let either the key or the book to ever fall into royal hands.*
>
>*We will be setting up perimeter defenses and traps on our way out. Without this book and the ability to use it, I don't see how anyone could ever find the cove or live long enough to see it if they got close. It's my hope that no one ever finds our little cove, but if they do, I pray to the Ancestors that they pay a bloody price to get there.*

After reading the last sentence, the words cleared from all of the pages.

She looked up at the map and text that said "Pirate's Cove" hovered over an arrow pointing to the southern point of the tiny isle of Eolan. She zoomed in and saw that the course to get there was treacherous. That region was famous for its diamond shoals, which shifted often and whose sands wrecked even the hardiest of ships.

Hailey asked the book, *Has anyone found Pirate's Cove? It's been two hundred years since she left it. Surely someone has been there."*

***NO.***

***I HAVE A RECORD OF EVERY SHIP'S PASSAGE SINCE THE EARLY DAYS OF THE COLONIES. NO SHIP OR PARTY HAS COME CLOSE TO THAT LOCATION SINCE RACHEL LAST DEPARTED***

Hailey looked up from the book to the map floating in the air. She looked at the tiny island of Eolan. It wasn't big, almost hard to notice, even though it was not too far to the south of the major seaport of Jakar. She wondered how it could be that no one had found the cove in all that time.

*So I have the only map to get there?*

***YES***

*And the only way to get in?*

***YES.***

*So how do I get there?*

The image pulled back enough to show their ship in the

air. A red line appeared on the map that zigzagged through the diamond shoals just off the coast, then up the river on the island. It was a complicated route. The flight there would be relatively short, but they would lose precious time once they got there. They would have to land. The cove was located up river on the island and surrounded with a heavy canopy of trees. The route was narrow and no doubt full of surprises, but they would have to risk it.

Hailey stood up from the bed and crossed the room. Dan, the sailing master, was just finishing his report on the rigging. He stopped mid-sentence as Hailey approached.

"I have our course, Captain." She laid the book down on the table. Everyone leaned in to look, but the pages were blank to them.

They all gave each other puzzled looks.

"You can't see that? I thought you just saw what was in the book earlier?" She pointed to the map floating in her vision.

"No. The book only talks to you. Only you can see anything," the captain said.

"But you could read what it said when I opened the book." Hailey cocked her head in puzzlement.

The engineer, Chloe, placed her hand on Hailey's shoulder. "I think that was something built into the book as some kind of verification for everyone. The book is keyed only to be read by someone in your bloodline. We can't see anything right now. Only you can."

The captain leaned forward in his chair. "So where is the treasure?"

"First we need to go to Pirate's Cove in Eolan and get the key. Once we have it, the book can tell me where the treasure is," Hailey replied.

"The diamond shoals, how fitting for the Queen of the Pirates," said Hadyn with a chuckle.

The tall, grim figure of the first mate, Olau, somehow managed to look even grimmer.

"That is a very dangerous passage, Captain." He turned and looked down on Hailey. "Can we fly there?"

"Only part of the way. The rest of the way, we will have to land and do some tight maneuvering, but a ship this size could manage."

Olau looked over to Dan. Had Hailey heard his earlier report, she would have learned that the sailing master had just spent the last three days changing the rigging for flight. Dan sighed and put his hands on his hips; the look of frustration was obvious on his face. He looked to the captain.

"We will have to change rigging again once we land to prepare for tight maneuvering."

The captain nodded and ignored Dan's frustration.

The eyes in the room returned to Hailey, who looked as if she was staring at nothing over the pages of her book.

"On our current course and heading, if we make adjustments, we can be there by mid-afternoon. I will give you the bearings and course."

The captain stood up and pushed back the chair, his height matching that of his towering first mate. The two together were unbelievably imposing.

Telos looked over at Olau. "Get everyone to their stations and prepare to head to Eolan."

Olau nodded, ducked his head, and moved through the door with a speed surprising for one of his size. Everyone began to follow and shuffled their way to the door. All except the captain, who stood watching them all. Hailey reached over to the table, picked up the book, tucked it under her arm, and started to follow the crowd.

"Hailey," the captain called to her. She stopped and turned to face the tall, dark, imposing figure of Captain Zordebran.

Hadyn and Kyra, who had been in front of her on the way out, hung back as well.

"Yes, sir?" she asked.

"Welcome to the crew of the *Dark Star*. You're one of us now." He slightly tipped his hat to her. She nodded her thanks and left the cabin with Kyra and Hadyn.

# CHAPTER 15

As Hailey predicted, they landed midday just outside of Eolan and began the slow trek inland. Hailey was thankful they had the book. Not only did it show her the way around the dangerous shoals, the book either deactivated or helped them to avoid all of the island's outer defenses, of which there were many. The waters were full of mines and the island itself was bristling with automatic cannons and even fire throwers. Even after all that time, the book registered that they all were in working order. Malik decided to test it out for himself. Seeing a mine just barely below the surface of the water some hundred yards off their port side, he decided to set it off. He took one of the long rifles and, after a couple of tries, he hit his target. The mine exploded, reverberating into a huge shower of water, turbulence that shook the ship, and shrapnel that fell just short of the hull.

"Yep. They still work!" he said, quite pleased with himself as he tossed the rifle to one of the automatons as he walked by the stunned crew, eyes wide at the size of the explosion.

Hailey and the crew now realized why no one had been on the island in over two hundred years. Without the book, they wouldn't have gotten within half a mile of the island before the defenses ate them alive. It was no wonder no one else had been there since Rachel had left over two hundred years ago.

She wished that they could have simply flown to the cove, but the map showed that between the shallowness of the channel and the thick foliage inland, flying was impossible. They made the slow trek to the mouth of the river that flowed through the island to the sea. There was still some breeze getting through the canopy of trees, but the current was against them and slowed their progress. Zordebran ordered the crews to break out the long poles to help push them along. Hailey zoomed in on their course as she stood at the front of the boat with her book and noted that they were surrounded by defenses every step of the way, as they made their way up the river. It was as if the woods on either side of them had teeth. Barely covered by the dense foliage, they could make out cannons that tracked their slow progress. They rounded a bend and saw several skeletons speared to trees through their ribs from one of the automated defenses.

Oddly enough, they didn't run into any trouble getting the tall masts through the ceiling of trees. Upon further inspection, Dan climbed to the top to discover that the foliage canopy was nothing more than an illusion of some kind, making them all wonder what was real or not in what they saw.

They eventually found themselves at the end of the river. It stopped at a pool just before a large waterfall that plunged down with great ferocity from a giant rock face above them.

"Is that the cove?" Hadyn asked.

Hailey consulted the map. "Nope." She pointed at the waterfall. "Through there."

Hadyn and Kyra shrugged at each other and signaled the captain and crew to push them into the waterfall. As they approached, Hailey and the crew watched as the water began to part for them, starting from the middle, as if it were a curtain. After the water had completely stopped, they could see what the waterfall obscured. Facing their black ship was a giant skull, its mouth opened up into a cave before them. The river continued into the darkness flowing from the skull.

As the crew slowly pushed the *Dark Star* forward into the mouth of the cave, Hailey could feel impatience welling in her to find the key. She felt as though she could explode in this mountain. Like the magma chamber of a volcano.

She didn't know if she could find the key and get to the treasure in time, but she was desperate to try. As they pushed on further, suspended globes from the ceiling began to light one by one, trailing deeper into the cave.

The crew feverishly worked the poles to push the boat up the mouth of the lit passageway. The passage gave way to a large, cool cave populated with several buildings.

They had found Pirate's Cove.

As they approached, Hailey got the impression of a city under glass, perfectly preserved. It looked as if time had forgotten the cave. There was a dock in perfect repair, complete with a boathouse. Several storehouses and cabins that dotted the interior looked as though they had been just lived in. Even the path to the main house, a two-story man-made villa that sat back on the rocks, was clear of debris, as though someone had swept it the morning before. Its appearance reminded Hailey slightly of the colonial mansion. It was enough to give Hailey the chills.

The lagoon in the cave was large enough for the ship to be able to turn around in. It took some time to coordinate the crews but once around, they pushed in to the docks easily, throwing lines along the pillars to hold them fast.

Olau was the first one on the dock to make sure that the

deck was as sturdy as it looked. The big, girthy man made it a point to jump around on the dock. He tested each board, as if the dock holding up the large pirate meant it would hold the rest of the crew without so much as a creak.

The captain left Hadyn in charge of the ship and the skeleton crew and told them to be ready to go at a moment's notice. The executive crew disembarked with Hailey to explore the cove.

Hailey tried to pace herself, but the image of an hourglass running out of sand kept pouring through her mind. More than a couple of times on the solitary trail that wound up from the docks, the captain and Olau had to pull her back behind them.

"Hailey, we don't know if there are any dangers ahead. You are the only one who can read the book. I'd prefer if you kept to the rear of us." The captain cocked an eyebrow at her.

Even on land, he was the captain, and to defy him was still insubordination, if not outright mutiny. It was better to be a part of the crew than in the custody of the crew. She felt her shoulders slump in surrender as the group slowly made their way forward.

Several of the buildings were storehouses, fully stocked with various types of supplies in large quantities. Rachel's crew could have resupplied for years with what was in those storehouses. There were even canned goods that looked to be still sealed and rust free. Hailey wondered if any of the crew were brave enough to test the canner's skill and discover what almost two hundred-year-old food tastes like.

The cove's armory was quite impressive. Everything from swords to cannons lay within, along with a full blacksmith's shop. The gunpowder was, of course, set farther back and away from any other building. Even though it was kept in a cave with a lake for hundreds of years, every powder keg was dry as a bone.

The longhouse looked as though a crew had just left. Just as in the cave earlier, every room they entered illuminated on their own by by suspended globes. Row after row of bunk beds, all looking recently slept in, filled the insides. There wasn't a speck of dust or decay here or in any of the houses that they had seen. The longhouse held baths, indoor toilets, and even a surgeon's station.

"Why does everything look brand new?" Hailey asked the group as they looked around.

"There must be something magic about the cave that preserves everything," Chloe said while looking around.

"It's a sterile field," Dr. Vinkler noted while examining the items found in the first-aid store. He was impressed; it was first-rate stock.

Holding up a small blade and inspecting it for rust, Dr. Vinkler made another observation. "I didn't notice any animals or insects, even under the rocks. Quite unusual."

"Does anybody think it's odd that every place we go a light comes on?" Hailey found herself staring at the orb suspended from a chain above them.

"It could be sensing our heat and turning on," Chloe said from behind her.

"What's powering it?" the captain asked Chloe.

Chloe followed Hailey's gaze and stepped closer. "I don't know." They all stood looking at one another.

"Maybe we should find out. Mr. Lucki, go with Chloe and help her find the source of the power. I want to know more about this place."

"But we need to find the key," Hailey said insistently.

"Agreed, everyone else with me." The captain turned to go, and the group was about to disperse when the doctor spoke up and stopped them.

"If it's all the same to you, I would like to stay and catalogue what is here. Our medical supplies have been dreadfully low, Telos. I think we might benefit from the resupply." Vinkler paused, looked down, and then back up at the captain and finished. "Sir."

"Wise thinking, doctor." The captain then turned to his first mate. "In fact, you and Chloe go look over the other storehouses first to see if there's anything we could use. Then search out the power source."

A small house stood on top of what looked to be a giant rock formation in the cave. The captain and crew found the walk up the path to the house to be steep but short. The house was a simple villa with an inviting wraparound porch with several benches for sitting and resting.

The group spread out and searched the house, going through room by room. Downstairs had living quarters, but no sign of a key. Hailey figured that the key would have to be with Rachel's things. Although it looked as if one of the occupants downstairs had been female, none of the group believed it to be Rachel. The clothes were too simple and utilitarian for that. The room was full of magic tools and odd manuals that they would inspect later. They had to get that key.

The captain led the way up the stairs to the landing at the top. The moment Hailey stood on the landing, that itching feeling in her brain went off. She felt as if a magnet were pulling her to the room to the right of the stairs. She pushed past the others and headed in that direction. The others wordlessly let her go and decided to check out the other rooms.

Hailey went to the door, slowly turned the knob, and stepped inside. The room burst into light and revealed a room full of color and vibrancy. The walls were covered in a fine crimson wallpaper that gave the room a rich, warm feeling. Cream-colored sheets and a cover shone through the matching mosquito netting on the elaborately carved, dark wooden bed, which looked comforting and inviting. Hailey crossed the room and noticed her feet sank into fine-woven carpet that covered most of the bright hardwood floors. She was tempted to take off her shoes and feel how sumptuous it was. This house, though similar in build to the colonial mansion, was radically different in atmosphere. It was a warmer and inviting place. Though she had grown up around homes formed from living trees, she felt that this odd man-made box contained just as much warmth and vibrancy as any living thing.

Still, like an iron filing to a magnet, she was drawn farther into the room. She passed the large closet, full of blouses and dresses of all kinds, each more lavish than the next. On the wall hung a portrait of a lady who looked remarkably similar to Hailey's mother. It must have been Rachel.

If Hailey had had the time, she would have appreciated the portrait more, but again the feelings of both time running out and being pulled along were too great.

She crossed the room and looked at a large desk that faced the wall. Several black mirrors lined the back of the desk, giving minimal reflection. Hailey had seen something like them in her travels to Crown cities. She couldn't remember what they were for. As she moved to the desk, Kyra came in behind her.

"Would you look at this room?" Kyra said. She spun around the room, wide-eyed.

"Uh-huh," Hailey said, distracted.

"Look at this carpet!" Kyra kicked off her shoes. "It's as soft as fur!"

Hailey focused on the desk. There were several hand-written papers scattered across it.

"Girl, look at this!" Hailey turned. Kyra held an outfit on a hanger at her. It was a black jacket with woven gold on it with a white blouse and long baggy black pants. Around the hook was wrapped a long red sash. "This looks as though it might fit you!" She smiled at Hailey.

Hailey looked down at herself and felt a little embarrassed. In all of the excitement, she had forgotten that she was still wearing boy shorts and the borrowed long shirt.

Hailey shook her head. "We don't have time for dress-up. I need to find that key!" Hailey slammed her fist on the desk, disturbing the pile of papers and sending a few to the floor. One of them caught her eye and she picked it up.

*18, Tredecim 5550*

*I have sent the book away for safekeeping, but I feel it pulling me, calling to me in my head. I think I have spent too much time with the thing because it even seems to invade my dreams now.*

*I am leaving the key here just in case. If I don't make it back, then my son can get it when he is old enough... if he becomes old enough. They have him in McKinnett now and have offered a trade, a trade I will have to take.*

THE NOTE REMAINED UNSIGNED, but Hailey recognized the long, looping handwriting of Rachel from the book. She turned back to the pages on the desk and looked around at the scattered papers, hoping to find something, anything, that would tell her more about this key. She had asked the book earlier, but it only would say that it was there, not what it looked like. She kept the book open just in case. Kyra set the clothes on the bed, looking disappointed, and continued going through the items in the room.

"Oh, wow! Would you look at this?"

Hailey looked up to see Kyra holding a sheathed cutlass

with a scrolling metalwork design on its hand guard. She unsheathed it, and its edge looked clean and sharp.

"This is mine!" Kyra said with a grin.

"Wrong." The captain strode into the room. "It's Hailey's." They both looked up at him, puzzled. "She's the heir to the Pirate Queen. By all rights, this is all hers."

Hailey stood by the desk, stunned.

Kyra sheathed the blade and put her hands on her hips. "You mean this girl is the new Pirate Queen?"

The captain grinned and nodded at Kyra. "It looks that way."

Hailey sat down at the desk, a little excited and scared at the thought. She had never thought of herself as anything special, just a girl who wanted to sail. Now she was the heir to the Pirate Queen and owner of Pirate's Cove.

"Did you find it yet?" the captain asked.

Hailey snapped out of her reverie and looked at him. "Not yet," she said, shuffling more papers.

"Then keep looking."

"It would help if we knew what it looked like," Kyra muttered and set the sword on the bed as well. Zordebran and Kyra circled the room, going through drawers and looking at the back of paintings, as Hailey combed through the pile of papers. She knew that the key was there. She could feel it just as she had felt the book. She glanced at her book on the desk. The pages remained blank.

She began to go through the drawers of each side of the desk, but all she found were more papers and files. Finally she checked the drawer in the center of the desk. It contained a few inkwells, a few quills, and a small, plain leather-bound journal. She pulled out the journal and noticed that there was something in between the pages and placed it on the desk next to her book. When she opened the journal, there was a gold bookmark on a page with only two words on it.

Good luck!

It was in Rachel's handwriting.

She picked up the bookmark and examined it. It was gleaming gold and seemed to radiate. Out of the corner of her eye she could see that her open book's pages were changing color from black to white. Without thinking, she placed the bookmark in the book. Symbols began to fly down the length of the pages only to clear and start again. After three repetitions of this it stopped, and the map flashed up into view over the book. The map zoomed in on an area in the northern sea known as the Sea of Mists. It glowed golden to her, and the map plotted out a course before them. She knew it then.

She had found the key.

Hailey gasped, and Kyra and Captain Zordebran came to her side.

"You find it?" he asked.

"I did!" Hailey beamed at him, then turned back to the map.

The image stared back as it floated before her. It was a giant golden mountain swimming its way out of the sea. Hailey had sailed the world with her father many times over and had never seen such a sight.

"Well, where is it?"

"It looks like an island to the north… in the middle of the Sea of Mists."

Zordebran watched her with interest as Hailey seemed to be staring into the air. "Not many ships venture into the Sea of Mists. Any ship entering the mists is more than likely to get turned around. The visibility is awful, and as soon as you enter the mists, your instruments go haywire. Mix in the odd winds, swiftly changing currents, and tiny islands and coral reefs that pockmark the area, and you have a place where no sane man or woman would go. It would also be the best place on Ephryae to hide a treasure."

Hailey zoomed out and studied the route the book projected. Captain Zordebran rested a hand on her shoulder. She looked over at him.

"If you have what you came for, we need to go, if we are to help your family." He quickly strode across the room and turned back to her and regarded her with a look a bit like pride.

"Perhaps before you join us, you might want a change of clothes." His dark eyes quickly flitted between the outfit on the bed and Hailey, then he left.

Kyra turned to her and said with a smile, "You heard the captain. Let's get you dressed."

THE SENIOR STAFF were standing on the docks trading notes about their findings but they all fell silent and looked when Hailey stepped on the dock.

She stood on the dock, book and bookmark under her arm, dressed in the clothes of the former Pirate Queen. They didn't fit as well as she'd hoped. The black pants were a bit long and flowing, and the white shirt, black vest, and jacket were a little large on her, but at least they didn't swallow her whole as her father's shirts had when she was younger. She liked the comfort of the outfit. It was something she could grow into or live with if she couldn't find a tailor. From her side hung the cutlass Kyra had found and on the other, a small pistol she'd found in the room, jammed into a long red sash that was tied neatly around her waist. Even though the outfit was baggy, she still looked stunning.

Everyone stood silent and ogled at her as she approached. She looked at them. "What?"

"Wo-ow!" Chloe stretched the word out for all its worth. "You look like paintings I've seen of the original Pirate Queen," Chloe said, grinning brightly.

Hadyn tried to say something to her, but it only came out as gibberish. Hailey looked at him briefly, smiled as she passed him, and went up the gangplank followed by Kyra.

"Close your mouth, lover boy," Kyra said to him slyly and nudged him as they passed.

The crew took their positions, and the *Dark Star*, freshly loaded full of supplies and gunpowder, pushed off from the dock and made its way out of the cave. Hailey stood at the bow of the ship, holding the book and reading the long list of traps and defenses around them. She looked up to the roof of the cave to see that even the cave had defenses. She could barely see the sets of spikes and gun mounts that would have greeted them if they didn't have the book. The whole island was bristling with defenses. Had someone been able to get to the shores and been foolish enough to set foot on the island without the book, they wouldn't have lived long.

With all those supplies and defenses, Rachel and her crew could have held out for years on the island. Hailey wondered if that had been their plan before the Crown took Rachel's son.

Hailey didn't have to look back to know the lights behind them went dark one by one as they passed. She was too busy looking at the curtain of the waterfall slowly opening before them. A few feet before the boat, the water stopped altogether, and they were back on the river.

The the crew of the pirate ship unfurled a few of her black sails to help the ship move down the river and back out to the shoals. Everyone on the crew knew that their time was running out and did their part to get them going.

Hailey gave the heading to Zordebran as they exited the cave and closed the book with the key inside for safekeeping. Her head was beginning to hurt a little from using the book so much. She placed the book in the pouch she'd found back in Rachel's room in the cove. The book fit so perfectly and hung so comfortably slung across her, Hailey wondered if that was what it was for.

The crews continued with their preflight routines as Hailey stood watching. The first mate called commands to the crew, as the captain kept his hands steady on the wheel. The skeleton crew stowed the long poles.

The sail master and his crew in the masts raced to unfurl all of the sails as they cleared the mouth of the tunnel of forest. Crews on the deck below rushed to the sides of the ship to release the two uninflated balloons attached on each side.

"Blimps away!" the first mate called, hand on the column. Chloe's voice could be heard responding from the column.

"Starting the pumps!"

A mechanical sound churned as the balloons slowly began to inflate from hoses that led from the sides of the hold. Hailey remembered getting a tour of it all from Chloe on their way to Eolan.

Below decks there were pumps that turned seawater into several things, including the mists. They also created freshwater and inflated the two large blimps with something that made them light enough for them to float away into the clouds. She made a mental note to see if she could get Chloe to explain how they worked again when it was all over. She'd tried to listen the first time but found her eyes glazing over a few minutes into the explanation.

Hailey made her way to the bridge and watched as the ship slowly began to lift from the water. As they slowly rose in the air, she felt her spirits lift. Hailey caught herself thinking that they just might make it in time and was hopeful.

A loud crack split the air, and a blinding flash of light erupted in the sky. The ship rocked and heaved heavily to the right. Hailey looked up.

One of the balloons had exploded in a giant ball of fire.

# CHAPTER 16

The *Dark Star* lurched to starboard and began to descend toward the water.

"What the devil was that?" cried Hadyn as he joined them on the bridge. The cant of the ship got steeper and steeper as they plummeted.

All but the captain stared, transfixed on the giant fireball above them. The captain steadied himself at the wheel, trying to maneuver the falling ship as best he could.

"Cut the lines!" Zordebran screamed.

Dan and Olau zipped into action, each brandishing cutlasses. They chopped furiously at the tethering lines to the balloon. They were soon joined by the skeleton crew, who hacked desperately at the cables. The captain tried to veer away as the last of the cables snapped, letting the flaming balloon crash down below them. Their one remaining balloon slowed their descent.

"Prepare for impact!" the captain shouted, and everyone dashed to grab hold of something solid.

The burning balloon landed in the water some feet away from them, blown by wind and tossed by the tide during their descent. As they hit, most of the crew were thrown off their feet. Hailey hugged a railing and the book with all her strength. The impact rattled her teeth and made her body ache.

The dark ship splashed into the water and bobbed violently, threatening to capsize with each rebound. Only Zordebran was on his feet, having clung to the wheel. Between the smoke from the fire and the mist machines still being active, visibility was awful.

"Report!" he bellowed as the crew began to recover and ran about the deck checking on their stations.

Olau came to the captain and gave the damage report, telling of structural damage and a few small fires from the burning scraps of blimp, but no casualties.

"I need to know what hit us!" Captain Zordebran shouted.

"I think we are about to find out," said Hadyn, looking over the starboard side.

As if to answer the captain's question, a Crown ship with a long steel coil crackling with lightning broke through the smoke and mists and slammed into the starboard side of the *Dark Star*, jolting the crew once again.

"Prepare for boarders!" Olau regained his feet and raced over to one of the weapons lockers that dotted the sides of the deck. He grabbed a boarding axe and hurried off.

The crew of the Crown ship had thrown hooks over the sides of the *Dark Star*, locking firmly in place. A sea of red-coated marines began to spill over the sides of the *Dark Star*. The skeleton crew were the first to greet them, wielding cutlasses and axes, but were quickly mowed down, their broken parts raining over the deck.

Olau waded into the fight, cutting and slashing as he went. Kyra followed up behind, dual blades flashing as she spun and sliced into the crowd. Then there was a huge cracking sound, and the middle of their mainsail exploded into splinters as it broke in half. A chain ball shot just under where Dan was perched. He dropped his rifle and clung to the mast desperately, as it and he plummeted over the side of the ship and into the water below.

On the starboard side, another ship appeared and closed in, this one much larger and flying the standard of the Queen. It fired again over the first ship aiming for the remaining masts.

Below decks of the *Dark Star*, Master Gunner Malik and his crew readied the cannons.

"Sir, we can't get the port side gun ports to open; the ship is too close!" said one of the gunners mates.

"Then fire through them! Alternate fire!" shouted Malik.

Every other cannon in the line roared as the wooden doors and a good deal of the hull vaporized. There were giant holes exposing the gunning decks on both ships now. The other ship had holes blown through and through, the bodies of their gun crews scattered over the deck.

Now they had a clearer view of what they were shooting at. One set of gunnery crews raced to reload the spent cannons, as Malik barked orders to the others who stood at the ready.

"Second volley, pitch down twenty degrees!" Malik intended to hit the crown ship below their water line and sink them.

His order to fire was nearly drowned out by the battle cries of marines pouring onto the *Dark Star*. They looked like ants spilling from a broken anthill as they ran through the gunners, hacking and shooting as they advanced.

Every other cannon fired, vaporizing the rest of the gunport covers, their shots striking home below the waterline.

The marines who had made it over from the first crown

ship forced them away from the cannons. The gun crews were no match for trained soldiers, and Malik knew it. He gathered as many survivors as he could and shouted for them to get above decks. Those who could still stand ran past him as he slashed open casks of gunpowder. When he reached the stairs he turned to them, grinned a devilish grin, and threw a match.

"Big boom!"

Malik was thrown up the stairs and onto the deck as the *Dark Star* shuddered from the force of the blast. Malik was singed but alive, his wild beard and hair mostly burned off. The surviving gunners gathered on either side of him and helped carry him to the bridge.

As they went up the stairs, the first crown ship began to pitch. Looking back, they saw that their shots had been true, and the crown ship grappled to their side was sinking and was starting to pull them down. Pirate and marine both abandoned their fights to slide down the sloping decks and cut the mooring lines of the rapidly sinking crown vessel. All of them chopped at the lines until finally the last line was cut, and the *Dark Star* bobbed back in the other direction. The ship pitched back and forth so violently that most found it difficult to stand. Once the rocking had stopped, they resumed their fight.

"Stay close to me!" Hadyn shouted over the din to Hailey.

She could barely see the others down on the main deck through the mist and the sea of fighting people. The larger crown ship was pulling closely along their starboard side. More troops from the taller ship dropped onto the deck like a great downpour.

The captain stood at the rails, pulling one pistol from his bandoleer and firing a round into the sea of marines before grabbing another one and repeating. One of the marines got off a lucky musket shot through the captain's thigh, causing him to falter. Dr. Vinkler hurried to help him as the captain fell to the deck and reached for another flintlock to fire.

Olau and Kyra were pushed back up each side of the two staircases by the marines' advance. Covered in blood and sweat, their tired arms swung and sliced away at the invaders. For each one who fell, it seemed as if two more would take their place.

Hadyn got in front of Hailey and held his sword at the ready, his two crossed pistols strapped on his back, as the troops advanced onto the bridge. The swarm of marines pressed them back to the rear of the boat. The doctor was dragging the wounded captain back with the help of Malik, and Kyra and Olau were taking defensive positions. They would not die without a fight. Hailey looked at the wall of muskets and rapiers pointed at them, slowly advancing, and knew the situation was hopeless.

Her blood boiled. This was not to be the end. All her life she was told to stand back, to let the men take care of everything. She was told that women had no place commanding anything; it was their job to accept and obey.

She could hear her Grandmother Rose telling her, *Surrender! Give them what they want. Your job is to serve the Crown. To serve, not defy the Queen and all her nobles. It will never change. Just accept things as they should be...*

"No, no, no!" Hailey shouted as she grabbed one of Hadyn's pistols from behind his back. She went around him and faced the wall of troops before her.

"Stop!" she shouted as she placed the pistol under her chin, preparing to shoot herself.

The troops stopped their slow press forward and stared at her blankly. They had been ordered to take her alive.

"You need me; otherwise, the book is useless to you! I am the Navigator! Let me speak to the one in charge." She looked over the stunned marines, searching for someone with authority.

As they stood quietly looking at each other, Hailey's heart and mind raced. She knew there would be a cost for her standing up and confronting them. But it was a price she was willing to pay. Too many people—her father, her grandmother, the pirates, and even her entire hometown—had been paying the price all her life. They were all in danger because of her. She couldn't stand by and do nothing. The Queen needed her alive. It was the only bargaining chip she had. She had to take the chance.

A slow clap broke the silence.

From behind the marines to her right, a familiar voice gave its reply.

"Bravo, young lady! Wouldn't your grandmother be proud, using your position to control the situation? Looks as if someone really was reading her primer."

Then the parting soldiers stepped aside to reveal the smiling face of Bishop Jacob Graver.

"Graver!" she snarled.

He stopped clapping, stepped through the row of troops, and raised his arm. The marines lowered their swords and muskets, but only slightly. Graver moved towards her slowly, but she raised the pistol under her chin slightly higher, staring at him, wide eyed. Graver took the hint and kept his distance.

"Yes, well, Her Highness sent me to work things out, since we have met before."

He motioned with his cane to the deck of the larger ship, where Hailey could see the Queen looking down at her. The Queen was wearing a flowing black dress with a partial veil that covered to just below her nose revealing pursed ruby red lips., Though her eyes were veiled, Hailey could feel her cold eyes staring at her if not through her. Hailey felt a chill.

Every member of the crew looked up at the Queen, stunned to see her. It was rare for her to be out of the capital, but to be on a ship of war was hard to believe. Zordebran tried to figure the odds of getting a shot off that would take her down, but it was no use. The Queen was just out of pistol range, and if anyone tried to raise a musket, they would be dead before the rifle touched their shoulder. No one dared make a move with that many muskets pointed at them.

"Met? Is that what you mean when you kidnap someone?" Hailey snapped at him.

"Well, we needed you and the book. I just took it upon myself to… expedite the process a bit."

Hailey frowned at him.

"Well, it seems that you have caused quite a stir since we last met. Towns rebelling, sinking Crown ships, even employing…" —he eyed the pirates with distaste and wrinkled his nose as he pointed at the pirates behind her with his walking stick— "this…"

"Hey!" Olau shouted at him, and raised his hooked arm in protest. "We're right here, you know."

The marines instantly brought their muskets to bear. The situation hung silently for a few tense moments.

"This doesn't look good. You have a plan?" Hadyn whispered behind her. She could feel his hand on her sash. Should trouble start, she was sure he would either pull her behind him or toss her over the railing to avoid the hail of bullets that would follow.

"I'm working on it," she murmured back to him, her eyes never leaving the bishop.

"Greeeeat." She didn't have to turn to see the sarcastic smirk that was no doubt on Hadyn's face.

Graver raised his hand, and the marines relaxed once again. All eyes focused on Graver and Hailey.

"I tell you what, there's an easy way out of this, you

know." Graver casually brought out an apple from his dark blue coat and began to polish it on his sleeve.

Kyra's stomach audibly rumbled as she watched Bishop Graver take a bite.

Graver bit into the apple with a crunch and savored it as he contemplated the bite on the skin. He seemed lost in the moment, forgetting the large squad of marines behind him or the girl with a pistol to her chin standing in front of him, or the Veiled Queen, who looked down upon them all.

Remembering himself, he grunted and continued. "You agree to come with us and give us the book and key. In return, we will let your friends go."

He grinned at her and looked quite pleased with himself as he took another bite of his apple.

"What about Daden?" Hailey looked at him doubtfully.

"Well, all right, them, too."

"And the plague?"

Graver's eyes widened in surprise, then his face fell back into his contented grin. "My, you certainly have been studying… very well. Come with us, and the plague goes away."

"This is way too easy," Hadyn whispered behind her.

There was a long silence.

"The way I look at it, we could either wound you and shoot your friends, or you can come with us, and we will let everyone go on their way." He shrugged.

Hailey couldn't see any other alternative. She didn't want the Queen to get her hands on the treasure or the book, but she didn't want to see her family and loved ones die.

"All right." She lowered the pistol.

"Excellent!" He crossed closer to her. "Now, do you have the book and key on you?"

She still held the pistol in her hand and turned the heavy barrel back to herself. "I'll give them to you when we are on board and my friends are safe."

He put his hands up and leaned back a little. "Fair enough." He held his hand out towards the port stairs, and the marines parted to allow them through. "After you."

Hailey turned back to Hadyn and gave him and the crew one last look before she passed through the crowd of marines to the gangway that had been extended between the two ships.

Graver leaned in to one of the marines and whispered something to him, which made the marine grin. The marine then smartly saluted him, and Graver made his way through the men to join Hailey on the ramp.

"They're gonna shoot us as soon as they get out of sight," Zordebran said through gritted teeth. The deck was heavily stained with his blood, and the doctor, for all of his work, was still having a difficult time staunching the bleeding.

"Well, at least we know she's safe for now," said Hadyn as he watched her ascend the gangway.

Kyra turned and murmured to them, "I, for one, am not planning to go without a fight."

"Nor I," said the towering Olau.

Now that the standoff was over, the crew noticed the mists had thickened significantly and were creeping up the sides of the ship. It began to act like a wall blotting out the world around the two ships.

Kyra took note of this and looked around. "Anyone see Chloe?"

Hadyn noticed an odd taste in his mouth, turned quickly to his crewmates, and told them, "Get your masks on!"

The crew looked around at each other and then to the marines, trapped in a moment of confusion. The marines looked back at them anxiously, ready to silence them and be done with it all.

Hailey had just reached the main deck of the Queen's ship, when she heard a crunching and the grinding sound of wood on wood. She turned quickly and saw that a long ship had cut through the fog like a spear and ground into the starboard side of the *Dark Star*. People jumped the decks from the ship and began engaging the marines. She recognized them instantly as merchants from her home port. One figure in particular stood out in her vision above the rest. It was a figure of a large mountain of a man who jumped from the decks of the *Arrow*, axe in hand, calling for his daughter.

It was her father, Orin.

Hailey looked back to the surprised face of Jacob Graver and attempted to run down the gangway to join her father. Graver reached out and grabbed her by her satchel bag to stop her.

Hailey turned, pistol still in hand, and pulled the trigger. Graver leaned back at the last second, and the bullet grazed his sharp cheek. Still he held on to the satchel, keeping her there in place. Hailey quickly slid out of the satchel that held her book and ran down the gangway, free from Graver but leaving the book behind.

Graver turned and held his hand over the running blood on his cheek, as he carried the satchel up the deck to the bridge, where the Queen waited.

Hailey plunged into the mass of heaving combatants, trying to weave her way to her father. She had to get to him, to see him once again. She had to know if everyone in town was safe.

She recognized several of the merchants as she wove in between the fighting combatants. They were members of her father's guild. Elbowing further through the crowd, she could see that several other guilds throughout the islands had joined the fray as well.

At the head of them, fighting their way up the port stairs to the bridge, her father swung his broad axe into a wall of marines, his long hair flying behind him as he hacked away at them.

Hailey cried out to him, but he couldn't hear her over the gunfire and the grunting and screams of those dying around her.

On the bridge of the *Dark Star*, the pirates were all wearing their masks, red eyes glowing as they fought back. She stopped and looked at them and then turned to notice that the mists were rising all around them. There was an odd taste in her mouth, much like the one she'd tasted the last night on the *Halifax*. Chloe must still be in engineering.

Hailey bolted to open one of the many weapons lockers and threw it open to reveal several masks. She put one on and breathed the fresh air that came through it. She then ran over to a group of merchants, telling them all to put masks on quickly.

The earpieces were alive and crackling, full of the sounds of those busy fighting or dying, it was hard to tell. She sprinted back to the locker to grab the remainder of the masks and made her way to her father on the bridge.

Graver looked down at the battle on the ship below while holding a handkerchief to his still bleeding cheek.

"Things do not go well," he noted out loud. He stepped back and turned to the marine who was standing there and said, "Send another detachment down there. Get the girl."

The marine saluted and hustled down the stairs to a large group of soldiers who stood waiting for him on the main deck of the enormous ship.

Hailey reached the bridge in time to see her father and the remaining pirates forcing the Crown's marines into a retreat.

Hailey ran up to her father, shouting for him. Orin stopped at once and turned to her, lowering his axe. She immediately embraced him.

"Hailey! I thought I had lost you!" He hugged her back.

"They have the book, Dad."

"Then we will get it back." He smiled at her.

At that moment there was a great shout as another wave of marines ran down the gangplank from the Queen's ship and began another push up the stairs.

"Stay behind me," Orin told her and ran forward with a shout. Those who could stand charged forward with Orin to repel the new wave of invaders.

They fought their way down to the main bridge, its decks slick with blood and oil and crowded with the bodies of marines, merchants, pirates, and the skeleton crew. Those fighting in the mess found it difficult to keep their footing. At one point, Hailey grabbed her father's belt to steady herself and wound up being dragged along behind him, her feet slicking along the decks.

"Graver's got the book!" Hailey shouted over the din.

Then the troops changed their tactics. Instead of attacking everyone outright, they concentrated their efforts in grabbing Hailey. Orin and the others caught on quickly and formed a defensive ring around her, as they slowly made their way to the gangplank.

"You and your dad get up there! Get the book! We'll hold them!" Hadyn shouted at Hailey when they reached the gangplank. The mists had fully risen about the ship and were starting to affect the maskless marines, making them slow and clumsy, but still they pressed forward to try and reach Hailey.

Orin and Hailey hurried up the gangplank. The mists had not reached that high, so they stripped off their masks to see clearly and not be distracted by all the voices of their crew-mates broadcasting through the masks. As Orin led the way, Hailey had the uncanny sense that they could do it. They could get the book back. There was nothing in their way. All the marines were too busy fighting on board the *Dark Star*. No one stood in their way.

No one except Jacob Graver.

Graver stood at the top of the gangplank, holding his ground as they closed.

"You go no further," he stated plainly and drew a pistol from inside his coat and pointed it at Orin.

Orin stopped. He was just out of striking range, and he wasn't sure he could close the gap in enough time before Graver got his shot off.

"A fine way to treat us after throwing you a party." Orin gave a sarcastic grin and looked Jacob Graver square in the eye. Had he been closer, he would have taken the man's head.

Graver tried to smile back at him, but the pain in his cheek forced him to wince instead. "Yes, thank you for that. It was quite lovely, but the whole burning the colonial mansion and running us out of town kind of spoiled it."

"Well, those things tend to happen when you kidnap someone's daughter," Orin said, unable to keep his tone civil. He tried to edge forward, but Graver was too swift and had the advantage of distance and reach.

Hailey peeked around her father, who stood there like a shield, and she held on to the ropes on either side of the gangway to keep her balance.

"I thought you said you would let us go," said Hailey with all the sarcasm she could muster.

"No, young lady, I said the Queen would let *them* go if *you* went with us," he said mockingly and leaned towards the two, pointing at her with his pistol. "*You* were the one who altered the agreement, and then *they*"—he swirled his pistol in the air pointing out the deck full of people fighting on the other ship—"decided to alter it more."

"So what are you going to do now? You can't open it

without me, and you are running out of marines." Hailey hooked a thumb back towards the deck.

Those marines who weren't dead from fighting were succumbing to the effects of the chemicals in the mists.

Graver smiled at the girl. "Oh, I think we will manage."

He motioned with his head to the Queen, who stood on the bridge, book in hand. The book's latches fell away, and the Queen slowly opened it, a smile appearing on her bright red lips. The map floated before her veiled face.

Hailey stood, stunned.

"If she can open the book, then why did you need me?" she cried.

"Well, we weren't quite sure she could open it. I guess she can," he said nonchalantly.

Graver looked at Hailey almost sympathetically and leveled his pistol at her. "We won't be needing your services anymore."

Orin gave a shout and lunged forward, axe in hand.

Hailey, screaming in panic, didn't hear the shot. She only saw her father's body fall forward and collapse on the gang-way. Hailey ran to him and dropped to her knees, wailing and shaking him as if he were only sleeping. He did not respond.

A storm of dark emotions washed over her in an instant, washing away the world around her as she clung to her father. From the back of his chest she could hear his heart was no longer beating. His lungs no longer took air. The man she knew and loved was gone. Lost. Taken from her just as her mother was, and there was nothing she nor anyone else could do. She sat with him, sobbing for her loss, clinging to him on the gangway.

Bishop Graver regarded them only for a moment and then turned and walked up to the deck as the *Virtuous* began to pull away. The gangplank slid off the edge of the ship, dumping Hailey and the body of her father into the water below.

They crashed into the water, sinking quickly. Hailey still clung to her father, his eyes wide open, frozen in the last look of surprise in death. His leg became snared by the rope of the gangway, whose heavy weight began to drag them down; a dark red ribbon of blood wafted from the hole in the center of his forehead and curled around them in the water.

It was all too much to take in. The book, the kidnapping, the pirates, and now her father was dead. As they sank deeper in the water, the light began to fade and the darkness almost looked welcoming to her. It was better for her to surrender herself to the darkness of the ocean's depths.

Above her, flashes of fire arced across the surface of the water, and there was a chest-shaking rumble, but none of that mattered to Hailey anymore. All was lost.

As she bowed her head in surrender, an arm wrapped around her waist and pulled her upwards. Hailey clung desperately to her father's corpse. She didn't want to let him go. Orin's body was still snared by the ropes and continued to pull them downwards. Hailey tried to hold on, but her grip slipped, and Orin's body dropped away into the deeper darkness of the ocean.

When Hailey and her rescuer crested the water, she gave a desperate gasp for air. She was angry at being rescued. She flailed to free herself from whoever rescued her and turned to shout at her savior. In the water with her was Hadyn. Looking into his almost hypnotic eyes, the hot anger melted away, and all she was left with was the cold feeling of loss. He glided over to her and gently put his arm around her and swam, guiding them both towards the *Arrow*.

Behind them, there was a terrible wet crunching and snapping and the final long moan of surrender that was the creaking death rattle of the *Dark Star*. Its hull was shattered and full of holes from the Queen's cannons. Slowly, as if a hand were pulling it under, the *Dark Star* slipped beneath the water like the ghost ship it was. The only trace it left was the sad belching bubbles as it joined Hailey's father in the dark depths below.

# CHAPTER 17

Still holding Hailey above water, Hadyn floated beside the *Arrow*. He had stopped his fighting, dropped his cutlass, and dove in after her when he saw the gangway drop.

Hailey's heart wanted to sink into the water and join her father below. Instead Hadyn had pulled her up and saved her. She was grateful to him for that, but some small part of her slightly resented him a little for doing it.

Hadyn grabbed a line someone tossed over the side of the *Arrow* and wrapped it around the two of them. Hailey didn't say a word as he pulled her close and looped the rope under their arms. Slowly they were hoisted out of the water and onto the deck where they were greeted by the surviving crew of the *Dark Star*. The crew wrapped blankets around them, and the doctor pushed his way through to check them over.

Hailey sat staring into nothing. She didn't know if it was water in her ears or if she'd hit her head, but the world seemed slow and muted. The crew around her were talking to each other, but she didn't know what any of them were saying. In fact, at that moment she didn't care. Her father was dead. She was alone.

Everyone looked exhausted from the fight. The *Dark Star* was gone, sunken beneath the sea. All the people who were left from the fight huddled on the Arrow's deck.

Hadyn stood next to Hailey as the survivors crowded around. Captain Zordebran stood resting on a crutch. Olau stood quietly next to him, his right eye covered with bandages.

The doctor knelt down to check Hailey's pulse, and she caught a glimpse of a scorched face behind him she thought looked like Malik, but with no hair. Beside him stood Kyra, who had her hand on her hip while she spoke to the group.

Missing from the group was the slender figure of the sail master, Dan Ellis, who must not have made it. Chloe sat on the deck, looking lost. It was the first time Hailey had not seen her smiling in the short time she had known her. As the crew shuffled past after being checked out by the doctor, Chloe asked about Dan. The tone of concern in her voice betrayed her hidden loss. She too had lost someone close to her that day. They all had.

So many losses, and for what, Hailey wondered.

Another merchant ship had finally caught up with the *Arrow* and pulled up alongside to lend aid to the survivors.

Hadyn and Kyra got Hailey up and helped her across the deck to the captain's quarters. She sat heavily on one of the chairs and made a point to not look back at her father's unmade bed or the picture on the wall hiding the cabinet where she'd first found the book.

She closed her eyes and tried to shut it all out. She wanted it all to go away. She wanted it all to be right, to have never happened at all. She had made the choices that led them there; she was the one who had taken the book. She had gone to Graver's mansion. She had gone with the pirates and taken them to the cove, where they had found the key. She had let Graver take the satchel with the book without a fight. The captain's hand turns the wheel, but it is the navigator who leads them where they are to go.

She opened her eyes to the group hurriedly conversing with each other. The door opened, and her father's first mate, Rufus, entered with the captain of the other ship in tow. It was her father's best friend, Seamus. Seamus stopped mid-stride when he saw Captain Zordebran standing, in front of him leaning against a crutch. The look of fear on Seamus' face showed that he recognized the form that had haunted his dreams at night.

Rufus placed a hand on his shoulder.

"Relax. They are on our side. How do you think we found them?"

Seamus remembered his last encounter with the pirates. He remembered the glowing eyes through the mists, the many skulls searching his ship, the falling into darkness. When he had awakened late the next day on the deck, the cabins and below decks had been ransacked, but he and his crew had not a scratch.

Rufus introduced him. "Captain Seamus Pike, this is my cousin, Captain Telos Zordebran of the pirate ship the *Dark Star.*"

Hailey's head whipped around, and her eyes went wide. Cousins? Rufus looked at her with his serpent- like gaze and smiled plainly at her as if to tell her *Yes, I was sent to watch you. I didn't like it either.*

Captain Zordebran limped forward and extended his hand.

"Former ship, I'm afraid. Nice to meet you. Sorry about before."

Seamus shook his hand. "Ah, well..." He trailed off, not knowing what else to say. "Say, where is Orin? Is he injured?"

"He is dead." Rufus lowered his head. "Captain, things did not go as well as we had planned."

Seamus stood stunned. Any man who had been to sea knew there was always a strong chance they would never return. Even though the thought had been evident to him after several years and countless examples of how life on the seas could be cruel, the idea that his best friend was gone pained him. He couldn't even look at Orin's daughter, Hailey, who still sat, wet and wrapped in a blanket, on the chair in front of him.

A moment of silence passed, and Seamus croaked out, "And the book?" He looked worried.

"The Queen has it," replied Zordebran.

Seamus's shoulders slumped, and he fought against the waves of despair in his heart.

"At least they can't open it. Not without the girl," Seamus said with a modicum of relief.

"She opened it," Hailey said flatly, and the room quieted. Hailey tried hard to not cry again.

Seamus's eyes finally met hers. "How?"

"Just before Graver…" She couldn't bring herself to say it, a lump in her throat prevented it. She cleared her throat and continued. "I saw the Queen open the book on her own. It can open for her. She can read it. She can see the map."

The room sat dumbfounded.

"I thought only the Navigator could open and read the book." Hadyn looked at his captain, but it was Chloe who answered him.

"Only a direct descendant of Rachel can open that book. That can only mean one thing: She is one as well."

No one knew much about the Queen. She lived her life behind a veil. She came from nowhere. The story propagated by the Church was that she had been a common girl from one of the colonies who worked her way up the social ranks and won the heart of the King. It was a wonderful story to tell the masses. It certainly helped to further reinforce their social order and give hope that any lady could advance that high.

The odd thing was that no one outside of the royal family, the high Church officials, or the noble advisors knew her name, only her title. The masses began to circulate a new name for her: the Veiled Queen.

Not long after the Queen's coronation, her much older husband, the King, had died, and she had found herself on the throne. There were many who said that she would take a husband and make him King, but she had yet to do so. The Church didn't press the issue, and when people asked, they gave the excuse that she was still in mourning these many years later, thus the dark veil.

Now they knew something else. She was related to Hailey.

"Did your dad or mom have any sisters?" Kyra asked.

"No, not that I know of, but my mom wasn't very close with anyone in her family. She never talked about them, and we never went to see them. I don't know." Hailey shook her head.

"Stars, I don't even know how I'm related to Rachel Feron!"

"Well, they have the book and the way to get the treasure," Rufus said, sounding frustrated. "What do we do now?"

"If we head to Daden now," said Seamus, "we might be able to break through the blockade and get some of the townspeople out before the plague hits." He looked at the pirate captain.

"There aren't enough ships to get through the blockade, let alone get everyone out," Captain Zordebran pointed out.

"In all probability, they are already infected," Dr. Vinkler interjected.

"We don't know that." Hadyn rested a hand on Hailey's shoulder and tried to look at her encouragingly.

"For all we know, they may have just released the plague when they formed the blockade," said Hailey, trying to cling onto some hope.

"If that's the case, we still might have time to get the device and stop the plague from taking effect," Dr. Vinkler offered.

Zordebran shifted on his crutch. "We have to go after the Queen. Nowhere will be safe once she is able to control that plague. She could infect everyone in the whole world without anyone's knowing it and choose who lives and who dies with the push of a button. I can't allow that. We have to go after them."

"But they have the map and a head start. We don't even know where they are." Seamus retorted.

Hailey remembered back to a time when she didn't know where she was. When she was on the *Halifax*, locked in the hold. She had felt the book's presence on the ship. In fact, she'd noticed from the second that she touched the book that it was a part of her, and she would know where it was. She shut her eyes and tried to feel for the book.

Somewhere in a dark corner of her mind, something pulled at her, like a compass pointing in a direction in which to go. She recognized that feeling, like an itch inside her head. It was the book. It was as if she could almost see it. She knew where it was.

"I know where the book is!" Hailey stood up and announced.

"But how?" Kyra asked.

"I can see it in my head." Hailey folded her arms. "Just trust me, I know."

Hadyn looked into her eyes and saw the fire in them.

Hailey wanted to save her town, but there was something more. Hailey wanted revenge.

She nodded at him.

"Well, she is the Navigator." Hadyn shrugged and looked at his captain. "Captain, I think we should go after them. It might be Daden's only chance."

"But what will we do when we catch up with them? She's on the biggest battleship in the fleet." Seamus was a good man and a good captain, but not a fighting man; he was a merchant.

"Yes, but they don't have much of a crew left," Olau said, breaking his silence while he leaned against the wall. The bandage over his right eye had a small dot of dried blood that almost made it look as if someone had drawn an eye over the one that was missing.

They all chuckled and nodded their heads in agreement.

Those of the Queen's marines who hadn't succumbed to the gas had fought fearlessly. The battle was still raging on deck when the *Virtuous* fired its cannons and rocked their ship. Those marines who hadn't died in the volley of iron and wood shrapnel jumped from the listing ship and desperately swam to try and catch their departing vessel. Those who were too wounded or were unconscious joined the *Dark Star* in its watery grave. Only a handful of marines were recovered by the merchants, and they were now locked in the hold of the *Arrow*.

Hailey took an impassioned step forward. "We have to go after them!" She could feel her face growing hot. The need for revenge burned within her. Revenge not just for her father, but for her mother, her grandmother, and her townspeople. Too many had suffered because of Jacob Graver and the Queen. She would do whatever it took to stop them, no matter the cost.

"Well then, Navigator, if you can see them, tell us where

they are." Telos Zordebran shuffled forward a little on his crutch and slowly and carefully took a seat in the captain's chair.

Hailey wove her way around the people in the cabin to stand in front of Zordebran. She unrolled the charts on the table, and everyone gathered around.

She looked up at both Rufus and Seamus. "Last reading, where were we?" she asked.

Seamus stepped forward and pointed to the map.

"Right here, not too far off the coasts of Eolan and Iconen."

Hailey placed a finger where Seamus had pointed and looked over the map.

"They were heading north by northeast when they left," Kyra added.

Hailey nodded and closed her eyes and let herself feel the pull of the book. Hailey was taking a big gamble, but she figured that this was how the Queen tracked them before, so she should be able to do the same. She marked their location on the map and, using a ruler and the pull of the book, traced her finger up the path along the ruler. She felt for a distance, her finger eventually stopping on an area full of symbols and warnings.

"They are here." She pointed to the spot on the map and looked around the room. The faces in the room fell on the news.

"She's already crossed into the Sea of Mists," Zordebran said.

They had hoped to be able to catch the Queen's ship before it entered the sea. With the book in their possession, they could have navigated through mists easily; they would instead be navigating one of the most treacherous places in the world, all based on some internal pull that Hailey alone could feel. She truly would be the navigator once they reached the mists.

"We can overtake them easily," grunted Rufus. Both he and Hailey knew that nothing on the seas could outrun the *Arrow*. They may have taken heavy losses, but with the surviving pirate crew they had more than enough hands to get under full sail.

"Yes, but what will we do when we catch them? Even if they are undercrewed, we are still outgunned," said Seamus.

Hailey, still stooped over the map, looked up at Captain Zordebran. When their eyes met, she cocked an eyebrow and Zordebran could see that a storm brewed behind those eyes.

"Captain, I have an idea."

# CHAPTER 18

The *Virtuous* pierced the wall of mists; the lights dotting the ship made it look like a tall lighthouse floating in the gloom. The Queen stood at the rear of the bridge. She studied the map and whispered directions to Jacob Graver at her side, who then relayed the information to the captain.

If it weren't for the lights throughout the ship, Graver wouldn't have been able to find the captain, who stood mere yards in front of him at the wheel of the enormous ship.

"Her Highness says to adjust course five minutes east, Captain. Steady as she goes."

Captain Jamal remained quiet but complied. Being a military man, he was used to taking orders, but not from civilians. Bishop Jacob Graver may have been the Queen's right hand man, but it was the opinion of the captain, as well as the rest of the marines, that they were the Queen's left.

Right now that hand was damaged, at least on this vessel. The captain had barely enough crew remaining to man the rigging; no one would be able to even aim the guns should trouble arise. The automatic systems were able to do things like rearm the cannons and raise and lower the sails, but humans were needed to make adjustments. There were too many places where a human hand was needed, and they simply didn't have enough crew members left from the fight.

After they were under way, the captain pleaded with the Queen and Graver to meet up with one of the other ships patrolling the waters of Eolan to recrew and resupply, but the Queen refused to hear his pleas. She demanded they get under way at once; she was confident they wouldn't face any more trouble.

Her captain did not agree. He did as he was told, but he didn't have to like it.

They were sailing into the most dangerous sea in the world, a place covered in mists where no instruments worked and there was barely a whisper of a breeze. He knew the ghost pirates weren't real. He'd seen them. He'd beaten them and sunk their ship. But the other myths and stories still lingered in his mind and those of the remaining crew. The childhood saying played over and over in his mind:

*Eyes of red*
*of the pirate dead*
*Are on the hunt for you.*
*Beware the mists,*
*And take no risks,*
*Lest you become a ghost pirate, too.*

THE QUEEN DIDN'T CARE about stories or feelings; she cared about getting what she wanted, regardless of the cost. Her ruthlessness was made clear when she ordered the captain to fire on the pirate ship loaded with her own people, a few hours before. She commanded it as casually as someone ordering a cup of tea.

Now the captain had only fifty crewmen, when he should have at least two hundred running the huge ship. Fifty men were not enough to go as quickly as they should, not enough to keep watch, and certainly not enough to defend themselves properly if someone should engage them. His thoughts turned treasonous.

Jacob Graver stepped to him again, which pulled the captain out of his contemplation.

"Adjust course seven degrees to port. We should be there soon."

"I'll do the best I can, but with no instruments and barely any visibility, it's hard to be sure," the captain grumbled.

"You won't do your best, you will do as you are told," Graver said, and with a turn, he stepped back to the Queen, who stared transfixed into the air just above the book she was holding.

Ahead of the *Virtuous*, the mists parted. Before the ship stood a mountain rising out of the sea. It was thick at the base and tapered off quickly to a curving spire, like a shiny thorn thrusting out of the water.

"My Queen!" Jacob Graver stepped forward with a face full of awe and wonder. "You have done it!" He turned back to her, but instead of the smile he was expecting, the Queen's mouth was open with horror.

Graver spun around to see a grenade exploding just above the main deck of their ship, and the concussion threw them to the deck. The crew of the *Arrow* sent out a cheer, as their ship turned away and moved back into the shroud of mists.

"How are they firing on us?" Graver bellowed at the captain as he struggled to get up. "They're just a merchant vessel!"

"That was a grenade, probably lobbed from a slingshot or

catapult," shouted Captain Jamal, his ears still ringing from the concussion of the blast.

Captain Jamal searched off of the port side with a spyglass, but it was useless. The mists were too thick.

"Well, find them and destroy them! This is a ship of war! One measly merchant vessel shouldn't be that much trouble!"

Captain Jamal turned in anger to Bishop Graver and snapped, "If we had a crew—"

He was stopped short by the approach of the Queen, who addressed him directly, her voice calm and even. "Get us as close as you can to that island, Captain Jamal. We will worry about the merchants later. Our first priority is securing the treasure." Then she turned to Graver and rested a hand on his shoulder.

"You and I will take one of the longboats and go to the sealed cave at the top of the spire. There I will claim my prize. Only the book can open the cave." She stepped toward him and brushed his cheek. "Don't worry, we've come too far to let those peasants stop us now."

Another grenade exploded above the decks on the starboard side, killing a group of men. The light from it was dazzling and left everyone blinking.

Another cheer from the *Arrow* went up as the ship turned back into the mists.

"Shoot at them!" Graver shouted in anger at Jamal.

Captain Jamal didn't seem to hear him. Instead he was focused on the figure standing on his main deck. It wasn't one of his crew—the clothes were all wrong. He knew there were no such things as ghosts, but there, staring up at him from the deck, was a giant man with glowing red eyes and a skull where a head should be, pointing a long, curved hook at him. On the rails on both sides, more glowing red eyes began to appear out of the mists. Captain Jamal stood horrified as if a childhood nightmare had just come to life.

"Aren't you listening to me?" Graver shouted at him and stepped over to the still frozen captain. Graver then followed the captain's gaze to see not just the lone figure, but several sets of glowing eyes rushing up the decks.

"Time to go!" Graver turned and ran to the back of the ship, shouting, "To arms! To arms!" to the almost nonexistent crew. Only a few marines were left on the ship; three of them broke off and boarded the longboat with the Queen to man the oars, as the others frantically sprinted down the decks to engage the boarders. Graver ran to join the Queen, as the pirates began to come up the stairs to the bridge.

"Stop them!" Hailey shouted as she and her allies ran onto the bridge. Hadyn and Kyra took the lead and began to engage the few marines who had taken up positions to bottleneck their progress.

Captain Jamal drew his sword and soon found himself face to face with the giant figure he had seen earlier on the deck. Jamal felt the terror in his blood, and his muscles ached with fear as he stared into the towering figure's glowing red eyes. It had just raised its axe to strike, when Captain Jamal blurted out, "I yield!"

The creature stopped its advance but kept the axe raised. Captain Jamal dropped his cutlass to the deck with a clatter and raised his hands as he ducked his head.

The massive figure of Olau closed the gap and placed his hook under Captain Jamal's chin, then leaned in close enough to smell the panic on the captain's breath.

In a low menacing voice, Olau said, "Smart man."

Hailey's plan to take advantage of the mists had worked. The lights around the *Virtuous* acted like a beacon broadcasting its location through the gloom. The crew of the *Arrow* could follow and close in, undetected. With the help of the pirate skull masks to cut through the mists and the bright lights that the ship was bathed in, the Queen's ship was an easy target.

Hailey and the other pirates had approached the ship in rowboats and waited for the opportunity to attack. While the Queen and her crew were distracted by the *Arrow* and the homemade grenades made by Malik, the pirates had thrown lines over the sides of her ship and quickly shimmied up the sides of the vessel, ready to fight.

As Hailey hurried to the bridge, she watched the wall of masked men and women clash into the line of guards like a great wave. They were no longer merchants, or members of a class, or even men and women anymore; the masks and the mists took that away. They were a people who wanted to save a town, avenge a friend, or wanted to be free from the rule of the Crown and to be in charge of their own destiny. If that made them pirates, then they were all pirates now.

Graver made it on board the longboat and shouted to the marine who stood on the other side. "Cut the lines!"

Graver then unsheathed his rapier and joined the guard in frantically hacking away at the lines.

The marines on the bridge were too busy trying to repel the mob of pirates to turn the cranks and lower the boat to safety.

Just as the pirates overpowered the last of the marines and broke through, the lines gave way and the longboat dropped to the water below with a heavy splash.

"No!" Hailey screamed. She ran to the banister and saw that the Queen and Graver were getting away. Graver smiled up at her and a waved.

Before anyone could stop her, Hailey mounted the rail and dove into the sea after them.

CHAPTER 19

The water was much cooler than the air above it that far north, but the fire in Hailey's heart burned so hot she barely noticed. Surfacing, she tossed off her mask and saw the longboat a few lengths in front of her, quickly making its way to the shore. She began to swim madly towards them. She didn't know what she would do when she caught up with them or how she would stop them; she just knew she had to get to them.

She had to stop the Queen from killing her people. She had to get the man who killed her father. She had to get that book back.

Though in her mind she didn't feel it, her muscles ached from both the change in temperature and exertion. With every stroke she made, it seemed that the longboat was pulling farther and farther away. It had been a while since she had to swim, a skill her father had been sure to teach her while living on the ship. She had forgotten how tiring an activity it was. Her energy began to drain from her, and she realized that she had made a terrible mistake. She struggled to keep her head above water but began to sink.

Hands plunged into the water and quickly pulled the semiconscious Hailey out of the water and onto a boat. Standing over her were Hadyn and Kyra.

"That's twice I've had to pull you out of the water today. Anyone ever tell you that there is a much easier way to get across water?" Hadyn smirked down at her. "Maybe next time you and your partner in crime won't be so quick to ditch me."

"Come on, lover boy, they're getting away!" Kyra elbowed him, plopped down on the bench, and grabbed an oar.

Hailey looked up at Hadyn smugly looking at her and allowed herself to smile at him. He tossed her a blanket and a small bag filled with dried fruit to help her regain her strength, then sat back down to his oar. Hadyn and Kyra began to row with all of their strength.

The blanket was warm and helped her regain her lost heat, and the dried fruit would help replace some of the energy she had expended in the water. As she warmed up, her muscles ached. She ignored the sensation. She had to push through and do her best to recover quickly. They were beginning to gain on the Queen's boat.

There was a loud crack and the hiss of a musket ball flying over their heads. One of the marines on the Queen's boat had stood and fired.

"They're shooting at us!" Hailey shouted, ducking low in the boat behind Hadyn and Kyra, who had their backs to the danger.

"Well, shoot back!" retorted Hadyn, bowing his head as he rowed.

Hailey panicked. "I've never fired a gun before."

"First time for everything. I don't have one, though," Kyra grunted as she rowed.

Hadyn grunted and rowed with all his might. "Reach

around me and take mine. Just point it at them and pull the trigger."

She felt awkward as she reached around him. He felt warm from all the exertion. The sensation felt good on her cold skin. She had never been this close to a young man before. He smelled of sweat and the sea. She realized she liked it.

*Hey! No time for that right now!* Hailey admonished herself for getting distracted and grabbed the pistol from Hadyn's belt.

She hoped Hadyn wouldn't notice how her face flushed when she sat back.

She looked the pistol over as they closed the distance. She had held the other one so readily under her chin before, prepared to pull the trigger and end her life to save others. Now she needed to take someone else's life to save others, and she wasn't sure it sat the same way in her conscience.

There was another crack and the hiss of a shot, this time much closer, causing Hadyn to jerk his head down reflexively. Their boat was almost on top of the Queen's. The standing marine was handed another musket to fire at them. Hailey steeled her resolve. Doing this was the only way to prevent them from being killed.

Hailey stood up quickly and pointed the pistol at the marine. She hesitated for a moment as she looked down the top octagonal barrel and pulled the trigger. There was a plume of smoke, a small spark of fire, and the loud crash of the shot.

Hailey peered through the acrid smoke billowing out of the pistol to see the marine falter, clutching his chest, and then he fell backwards over the side of the longboat with a splash.

Hadyn stopped his rowing and turned to watch as the marine dropped into the water. Hailey stood and stared at the place where the marine had gone under, her arm still outstretched, smoking pistol still in hand.

Hadyn looked up at her and said, "Nice shot."

The marine who had been reloading the musket popped up and got a shot off at Hailey. He missed wide to her left, but it was enough to snap Hailey out of her daze. She tried to pull the trigger again, but there was nothing loaded.

"Get down!" Kyra shouted. "You need to reload it."

"How?"

Hadyn sighed. Hailey knew that explaining it would take precious minutes. Precious minutes were things they didn't have. They had to keep rowing in pursuit.

"Switch with me," Hadyn told Hailey, and he abandoned the bench for the floor of the boat. Hailey took her place on the bench and handed him the pistol.

Hailey grabbed Hadyn's oar and began to row in time with Kyra, pulling with all her might. Her muscles still protested, but she could row.

Hadyn sat low in the boat and quickly pulled a pre-rolled charge and ball from the pouch on his belt. He reloaded the pistol with expert timing, rammed down the shot, and looked back up at Hailey.

"Okay, switch back."

Hailey released the oar and dove back to the floor. Hadyn handed her the pistol. Taking the pistol from him, an odd question crossed her mind.

"Hadyn, why don't you take the shot?"

He sat back on the bench and grabbed the oar. His muscles flexed tightly under the strain of the row, and his eyes would not meet hers. "Because I row faster and you shoot better."

Hailey knew that there was something else, something not being said. These two knew they needed the Navigator alive if they were going to get the treasure. It was better to arm and shield her behind a pair of bodies than make her a target.

They had almost caught the Queen's longboat. The Queen and Graver were out of sight, likely cowering in the boat, behind the two remaining marines. There was a shot, and a musket ball splintered a rail on the front of the boat, just missing Hadyn, making him shout in surprise.

Hailey peeked up and saw she didn't have a shot at anyone except the marine rowing. She thought twice about standing up and taking the shot, when she realized the other marine was peeking out from behind him with a rifle ready.

The bow of their boat slammed into the back of the Queen's boat, knocking the shot of the marine just wide of Hadyn's head; the musket ball hissed by Hadyn's ear. He cried out in surprise and cringed as he dropped his oar.

Kyra dropped her oar, sprang up to the front of the boat, and drew her long knives.

"Stay behind me, pretty boy." Kyra flashed a wicked grin at him and crouched at the ready. Hadyn knew better than to argue with her, especially when she could smell a good fight. She may have been a woman, but she was as fierce as her flaming hair. He got up from the bench and crouched behind Kyra in the front of the boat.

Hadyn turned and shouted to Hailey, "Row! Now!"

Hailey tucked the loaded pistol into the front of her belt, next to where she kept her deck knife, and leapt onto the bench. Grabbing both oars quickly, she leaned back and heaved with all her strength.

Their boats bashed together again with such violence that one marine careened into the other, sending them both tumbling to the deck of the longboat. Kyra, quick and agile, took the opportunity to leap over and advance on them.

Graver popped up from the front well and grabbed the closest marine.

"Row, damn you!" he yelled and jerked one of the marines off the other and onto the bench.

With every stroke they closed on the shores of the golden spire. No wind disturbed the waters, no waves rocked the boats. The flat, glassy plane of the water was sliced only by the cresting wakes of the two boats rapidly advancing.

Kyra and the standing marine clashed awkwardly at the back of the Queen's boat, sending it rocking perilously as the other marine watched helplessly and rowed.

Finally the Queen's boat slammed into the soft silt at the base of the spire with a jolt. Kyra fell forward, knocking down the marine she was battling with as she went. The momentum of Hailey's boat carried them crashing into the stopped boat and rocked the passengers violently. Hadyn leapt over to the other boat and quickly engaged the last marine, who rose up, oar in hand. Graver and the Queen were at the front of their boat. They fumbled unsteadily over the side and onto the soft, mucky silt of the spire's shore.

Hailey watched the two of them as they trudged their way up the beach, their feet pulled down by the muck with every step.

She couldn't let that happen, she couldn't let them win. Hailey vaulted onto the other boat. Ignoring the others, she raced past the struggling combatants, leapt over the side, and quickly sank into the muck up to her shins.

She cursed as she fought to free her legs and slog her way out of the water. Once on shore, she could see that the two ahead of her were having more difficulties. The patch ahead of them was soft and slick. From the amount of gray muck on them, Hailey judged they had fallen several times and finally resorted to crawling their way up.

Hailey made her way cautiously up the slippery slope to join them. She was close enough to stand over the out-of-breath Graver, who rolled on his back to greet her, his long rapier in hand, pointed at her.

"Well, you are persistent. I give you that," he said.

"I should end you now."

"We'll see about that."

Hailey reached back to pull the pistol from her sash, but it was no longer there. She must have dropped it while she was making her way to graver. No matter, she still had a sword.

Hailey drew her cutlass from its sheath and advanced on the prone Graver. She didn't know much about swordsmanship, but she knew that if you stabbed someone enough times they would eventually die. The man man who had killed her father deserved that much.

She advanced and tried to thrust her blade at him, but his rapier had the longer reach, and he batted each strike away. Graver took advantage of her imbalance and kicked out her leg, sending her crashing into the foul-smelling muck facefirst. She could taste the grit of it in her mouth, and it made her spit. She looked up and rolled fast enough to escape Graver's blade, which came down right where her head had been.

Rolling away, she dropped her cutlass. She sat up, panicked, looking desperately for it. Her head felt heavy, for her long-braided hair seemed to have sucked up pounds of the sludge when she rolled. She was covered in the slick stuff. She was on her hands and knees, searching around and helpless, as Jacob Graver knelt over her and raised his blade to deliver the killing blow.

In that moment, Hailey's heart sank. Was this it? Was this the end? Had all their struggles and losses been for nothing? The Queen would win, Hailey's town would die, and no one would ever know anything different except the heavier and more repressive heel of the Queen on their necks.

The blade began its terminal arch towards her. She shut her eyes.

She heard a thud and a scream of anger. Hailey opened her eyes to see Hadyn on top of Graver, the two wrestling in the muck.

Hadyn's eyes found hers, and he shouted, "Go!"

Hailey nodded quickly and began crawling her way past the two wrestling men.

"This isn't over, young lady!" Hailey could hear Graver shouting. She found herself agreeing with him as she climbed the slope. It was far from being over between the two of them.

The Queen was well ahead of Hailey, having made it to firmer ground. The land was no longer covered in the smelly, slick muck, but instead was replaced with what looked and felt like an odd, gold-like metal.

At the edge of the muck lay a filthy crown with a veil attached to it. Hailey looked up to see the Queen just ahead, her back to them all. Her once black dress and raven-black hair were now slicked with the gray silt.

"Stop!" Hailey shouted at her, when she caught up. "Why are you doing this?"

The Queen stopped her slow advance. Hailey could see she was now barefoot. The Queen chuckled and said casually, "Because it is what a lady is expected to do, silly child."

She turned and Hailey froze, her mouth hung open in disbelief.

"Mom?"

# CHAPTER 20

They stood silently. Hailey stared as the woman with her mother's face looked coldly back at her.

"No. I'm not your mother, you fool. I'm her sister. Her twin sister." The Queen feigned a hurt look and cocked her head. "What, she never mentioned me?"

Hailey fumbled for words. Her mother had never talked about her past. Hailey hadn't stopped to wonder why. It dawned on Hailey that this explained Graver's odd looks. He knew she was related to the Queen. The Queen looked like an older, darker haired version of Hailey.

Hailey tried to say something, but no words came when she opened her mouth. She could only shake her head in reply.

The Queen gave a knowing chuckle and sneered. "Didn't think so." The Queen arched her eyebrows and began to pace back and forth on the edges of the path, cradling the book under her arm like a child. With each pass she grew more and more agitated.

"You want to know why she never mentioned me?" She spat the words like venom at Hailey. Hailey flinched.

"Because your mother was a disgrace!" she shouted.

The Queen began to pace more rapidly, growing more agitated. The more she talked, the louder her voice got. The woman was clearly unhinged.

"I tried to be the good daughter, tried to be a proper lady and advance us. And did my sister even try? No! She was too busy being independent and running off with some common merchant!" She tsked and continued her rapid pacing. "Even though they said I was the 'special one,' they talked about her endlessly after she was gone."

Seeing how deranged her aunt was getting, Hailey wondered just what her grandparents had meant by 'special.'

The Queen continued. "I grew to despise her. She broke the rules! She forgot the order of things, and look what it got her. Doomed to a common life, with a common merchant, and a common child." She sneered at Hailey. "I clawed and I scraped my way up the social ladder and look at me now! I'm the Queen!" She leaned toward Hailey and pointed at herself, laughing and flashing a manic grin. Hailey was only a few feet away now. The Queen liked to talk. All Hailey had to do was keep her talking.

"S-so how did you know about the book?" Hailey quietly asked the crazed figure before her.

The Queen held the book out to her. Hailey could feel its pull, as if pleading to take it away. "This?" The Queen bared her teeth. "I was the Navigator before you! Your mother stole that from me! She stole my book and sent it away. She and your father gave it to those pirates to hide it from me, but I knew it would eventually work its way to the next heir. So all I had to do was sit and wait until it got itself to you. Then I could take it back, and so I have! It is mine!"

The Queen's eyes were wide, and her face pulled back into a smile that almost resembled a scream.

"It is my right! I am the eldest daughter; by all rights it is mine! This book has been passed down in our family to the oldest daughter for hundreds of generations, long before even Rachel's time."

Hailey's face betrayed the recognition of the name of the first Pirate Queen.

"Yes, I see you know about her, too! Hers was the first name I struck from the history books after I assumed the throne. I couldn't have anyone upsetting the order of things, could I? I mean the very idea. Colonies rebelling? Sanctioning pirates? Crowning a queen who hadn't earned her place?"

"So you subjugate women because you want order?"

"No. I manipulate and control with order. I subjugate both men and women with rules. Rules I made and, thanks to Jacob, the Church teaches and enforces. He's such a jewel, Jacob Graver, but you have discovered that, haven't you?"

She didn't call him Bishop, she called him Jacob. She sounded far too familiar with him. Just how closely did they work together? The Crown and the Church had been collaborating for some time, but Hailey hadn't suspected this degree of intimate cooperation before now. The Queen looked down at the book and placed a hand on it, almost petting it. Hailey edged closer.

"Rules can be such cages, can't they?" she breathed affectionately. "The rules on women affect men, too. Not many a man out there wants to displease his wife, now does he? My poor late husband didn't. He died trying to please me. At least I have his throne. It's what I wanted most in life, after all. Well, that and this book. Now I have them both!"

The Queen didn't need to say it. Hailey could see from the glint in her eye that her husband's death had been no accident. The Queen had killed him, and given the means, she would kill Hailey, too.

The Queen held out the book and looked at it excitedly,

then embraced it. Hailey gritted her teeth at the sight of this evil woman hugging her book.

She blurted out, "Did my mother know it was you on the throne?"

The Queen resumed her pacing and thought for a moment before she spoke. "I'm sure she suspected. But she was too wrapped up in her new life to think about anyone in her old life like our family. You know she left our parents all alone?" The Queen shook her head and looked at her. "You see, it's the duty of the youngest daughter to take care of the parents as they get older. Granted, I was only a few minutes older than my sister, but still I was the older one. That's why I got the book, and she was supposed to watch our parents, but she decided to change all that. She stole the book and left me there to take care of our poor parents alone. I'm sure they were crushed." A malevolent grin showed on her face. "I ended up taking care of our mother and father not too long after your mother left." She looked away wistfully. "They died quietly..."

Hailey felt anger, hatred, bile rising up in her. "You killed them?" she said through gritted teeth.

"Yes." Her icy grin didn't waver.

"And the King?"

"Yes," the word hissed out of the Queen's lips like a serpent.

"You killed my mother, too." Hailey balled her fists. Her anger rising.

"Yes, I did! At Cowl's Ridge!" She licked her teeth, her mouth wide in glee. "When I found out she was in that rebellious little town, I thought it the perfect opportunity to try out one of the toys I had found in the vaults of the capitol. I had read about the plague in the book when I was younger, and I was excited to see what would happen. I was going to do it anyway. Your mother was simply a wonderful bonus!"

"You murdered her! You murdered all those people!" Hailey screamed and lunged at her, but she was stopped short. A hand grabbed her braid and held her back. It was Jacob Graver. Hadyn was on his back trying to pull him off, but still Graver held her fast. Hailey screamed in pain and frustration, as the Queen turned and started up the path to the top of the spire.

Graver tried to pull Hailey back down the slope by her hair. Hadyn, still slick with muck, tried his best to pull Graver back down to the ground, but Graver's long limbs were planted firmly, and he kneeled in place. In desperation, Hailey reached into her belt and grabbed her deck knife. Though the blade was short, it was sharp enough to slice through the thickest ropes. She quickly reached back behind her. Graver's hand was too far away to stab. But she had to get free, to stop the Queen before she got to the top. Hailey did the only option she could—she sawed at her braid.

The hair quickly gave way to the sharp blade, jerking her head violently forward once she was free. Graver still clutched the braid of hair, as he and Hadyn fell back into the muck and slid down the slope.

Hailey sprinted up the path and tackled the Queen from behind, sending the book sliding away. The steep slant took them all back down to the muck, where Hailey and the Queen wrestled. Hailey was smaller, but she had spent her entire life on a ship, not lounging at tea parties. Her muscles were long, lean, and powerful from her many years of climbing rigging and hauling lines. Hailey pinned the Queen's shoulders and drew her fist back to punch her aunt in the face.

The Queen lifted her head up, spat a bit of the muck at Hailey and said, "Better hurry up! Everyone else you love is about to die."

Hailey paused, her fist still hovering in the air. "What do you mean?"

The Queen rested her head back and started to laugh. It was the kind of laugh that made Hailey's stomach hurt because she knew something was wrong. Then she felt something trickle from her nose. She reached up and wiped and saw that her fingers were covered in dark, rich blood.

"You are infected, too!" the Queen said, laughing. "In fact I infected your whole town when I found out the book was headed there. They were serving more than just cocktails at your party in the colonial mansion!"

Hailey's eyes widened in panic. The Queen continued laughing.

"You like that? Even better, all your pirate friends are infected, and they'll die too!"

"But I thought it takes several weeks to work?" Hailey looked at the Queen with horror.

"Is that what your pirate friends told you, sweetie?" the Queen said with a laugh. "Well, they were wrong."

The sick feeling in Hailey's stomach started to spread throughout her body. A dull throbbing ache seemed to radiate from her bones outward to her skin. Her body gave an involuntary shudder. The Queen suddenly stopped laughing and raised her head, her cold brown eyes locked with Hailey's as she spoke.

"You can spend your last few minutes fighting with me or you can go get the cure. Which is it?"

Hailey wanted to end it, to end her. She felt sicker and sicker every second that passed. But did she stop there? How did the plague even spread? For all Hailey knew, everywhere she'd been and would go, a swath of death would trail behind her if she didn't find a way to stop the plague. Everyone she touched, anyone she had ever been around could be wiped out.

Hailey punched the Queen hard in the face, knocking her out. Slowly, Hailey crawled on hands and knees to the book, which had slid into the muck a few feet away. Book in hand, she glanced back at Hadyn. He was still struggling with Graver, trying to keep him pinned on the ground. Hadyn's face was almost as pale as his eyes, but his look implored her to go on.

Hailey tried to ascend the spiral path quickly, but it was slow going. With every step, she felt more as if her body were about to fall apart. Her ears rang, her nose bled, and her head felt as if it were on fire. Still, she trudged up the path of the steep spire. Close to the top of the path was a large opening. All she had to do was reach it.

She was tired. Her legs were weakening. Her body kept telling her over and over again to stop. She put one foot after the other, but her feet felt full of lead. She fought onward. It wasn't that far up, but in her condition, it may as well have been miles.

Halfway up, she faltered and dropped to her knees. She couldn't find the strength to stand anymore. She had tried her best, but the Queen had won. Her body was failing her. She had failed everyone. Hailey sank her head to her chest and began to breathe heavily.

Behind Hailey, a hand reached around her and lifted her on her feet.

"Come on, girl. I've got you."

It was Kyra. Her face was bruised, she was covered with muck, and her bright red hair was plastered with the gray silt. She smelled like a latrine after fighting the marine in the muck and looked like she had been she had been dragged around by her face, but Hailey knew she looked far better than the marine she had fought. There was no doubt that he was probably lying somewhere dying or dead.

"Come on, we have a treasure to find." Kyra urged her

slowly forward, up the steep grade. Hailey nodded her head loosely and set one foot in front of the other.

Hailey had no idea how to stop a plague that was killing her and her friends, but she had to get to the top and try. The cure was up there somewhere. The two slowly ascended the path of the spire to the top. Hailey glanced back from time to time, but no one followed. At the top, they found themselves at the mouth of what they thought was a cave, but upon closer inspection Hailey saw it more closely resembled a vault. Its giant face, though recessed, was smooth and metallic, save for what looked like writing in some strange language carved into it. Only two large metal doors stood between them and salvation. Hailey and Kyra both tried to push them open, but neither was strong enough. The doors would not budge.

Hailey's strength was quickly failing her. Her body began to sag. It took an amazing amount of energy just to turn her head and look at Kyra.

"How do we get in?" Hailey asked.

"I don't know, ask your book!" Kyra's breathing heaved, and she sat down on the ground beside Hailey.

The book! In all of the excitement, she had forgotten that she was carrying it. Hailey's arms were almost as numb as the rest of her. She sunk to the ground with Kyra and placed the book on her lap. The latches fell away, and she opened the cover.

Hailey asked between painful breaths, "How do I get in?"

### *ALL YOU HAD TO DO WAS ASK*

She looked up at the doors.

There was a deep rumbling and then the crashing and clinking of metal that had not moved for over two centuries. The doors parted and slid open silently. Inside, it was cavernous and dark. From the front to the back, as in Pirate's Cove, lights began to wink on one by one, illuminating a vast cave filled with treasures.

"You did it! We're in!" Kyra shouted.

Hailey ignored her and continued talking to the book.

"How do I stop the plague?"

It was getting harder for her to breathe. Her words came out in gasps.

Two words appeared on the pages blinking over and over again.

## *ONE MOMENT*

Hailey felt queasy, and her head began to spin.

The page changed, and a drawing of a long cylindrical tube that looked almost like a pen or a small spyglass with several buttons on it appeared. Below the image was written,

*LOOK FOR THE DEVICE INSIDE.
IT SHOULD ONLY BE A FEW PACES INTO THE CAVE ON
THE RIGHT.
RACHEL LEFT IT ON THE LECTERN.
ONLY THE NAVIGATOR HOLDING THE BOOK CAN
ENTER THE CAVE FIRST. HURRY!*

Only Hailey first? There must be some kind of a trap for anyone other than the Navigator. She would have to go alone.

Hailey didn't have the energy to hurry, but she would try. She mustered up what was left of her strength and pulled herself up. Kyra tried to join her, but Hailey waved her off. Kyra looked at her, puzzled, but Hailey turned and plodded into the mouth of the cave. She had to go first. There was no telling what would happen if Kyra went with her.

Covered in sweat, eyes losing focus, Hailey urged her body to keep moving. Every step felt like an eternity. She searched the room. Piles and piles of gold, jewels, and magic tools lay sprawled all over. In the middle stood a lectern. She went to it and resting on the lip of it was a small cylinder that looked like the drawing in the book. She picked the device up and placed her book open on the lectern, hoping to read the next set of instructions, but she couldn't. Her eyes refused to focus. She squinted and tried, but she couldn't see the words. A low groan escaped her drawn-down mouth.

From somewhere in the lectern, a pleasantly calm male voice floated up to her. It startled her at first, but Hailey knew exactly who was talking to her. She had heard that voice before. It was the one she didn't recognize in the square, the same voice she heard in her head every time she read the book. Now that voice spoke to her and said,

**_WELL DONE, HAILEY! NOW PRESS THE SECOND BUTTON ON THE TUBE._**

She couldn't focus her eyes, so she fumbled her hands over the device, searching for the buttons. She could feel her pulse in her neck, and it was getting harder to breathe. She found the buttons along the cylinder and pressed the second button.

She felt a jolt like lightning through her body. She pitched forward and convulsed as her body spasmed. Hailey crashed to the floor, and her head swam into darkness.

# CHAPTER 21

*H*ailey was surrounded by light. She stood in a room that was warm and inviting, even though it was vast and empty. She turned about slowly, and upon returning to where she started, found herself facing an older gentleman.

His face was clean shaven and betrayed some wrinkles of age. The crown of his head was bald, wreathed by short white hair that stretched around the back of his head from temple to temple. He was tall and lean, not muscular. The most peculiar thing about him was his eyes. They were a color she had never seen before, as blue and bright as the sky. He stood with his hands clasped behind his back, his face turned up in a mild grin, as if patiently waiting for her to speak.

"Did I do it? Are they safe?"

The figure looked amused. "Yes, dear. You did it. Everyone who was infected by the nanites was saved. Better than saved, actually."

Hailey looked at him, puzzled. Nanites?

"It wasn't really a plague that affected people; it was more like tiny automatons run amok in their bodies. The nanites' job is to fix people, not hurt them. I'll explain more about it later, when we have time."

She felt oddly at peace. She looked around the brightly lit room, listening for any sound but neither saw nor heard anything else, not even a whisper of air moving. She could only come to one conclusion. Hailey let out a gasp.

"Am I…" Hailey stopped and let the words drop.

"No, no, no! You are quite alive. I simply borrowed you for a moment. We are in a room inside your mind as your body recovers, that's all. I thought it was time we meet."

Hailey recognized the figure's warm and soothing voice, a voice she had heard only moments before.

"You're the book," Hailey gasped.

The man cocked his head and glanced to the side as if to think about it for a moment and then replied, "Well, yes, in a way. I'm certainly a part of the book, but I'm a bit more than that, you see. I am a bit too large to be contained in just one small volume." He winked at her and his eyes seemed to glow.

"Then there are more… of you? More books?"

"Well, not just books. I am in many things, really. In fact, you opened my door and stepped inside."

Hailey's eyes went wide. "You mean you are the spirit of the cave?"

The figure chuckled at that and shook his head.

"Spirit of the cave, how funny…" He looked at her, amused. "Yes, I am part of the book, this cave, even this whole place you think is an island, but I'm not a spirit. I am a program." The figure noted the expression of confusion on Hailey's face. "Think of me as a machine. My name is Lucien."

"So what is this? Why is it that I can see and hear you now? Why haven't you appeared to me before?"

"Well, it took some time to bond with your mind. It usually doesn't take long, but you didn't have the book in your hands very long. Anytime you did have it, you were always having it taken from you." His eyes twinkled as he smiled at her and continued. "Over time we formed a bond that makes you receptive to communication with me without the book. If you are here on this island, I can appear to you inside your mind. It takes a lot of energy to do, so we have to be where my energy is the strongest."

"So why do we need to meet like this? Is there something you need to tell me?"

He tilted his head and pursed his lips a bit as though thinking.

"Tell you, yes, but better than that, show you."

He extended his hand, and the room went dark. Beside him, a large blue sphere appeared, smeared and dotted with whites and browns that lit the space and cast a warm reflected glow on them both. It was a highly detailed view of Ephryae, spinning alone with them in the dark.

He looked over at her, pleased with himself as Hailey watched with fascination. Lucien dramatically swept his arm, and the globe expanded around them and through them until they were in the center of it all. Everywhere she turned, there was her world as a globe spinning around them. She was actually *in* the map.

She stood, gaping. She found it hard to take it all in. She didn't hear Lucien walk over and stand next to her.

They both stood as the world turned around them.

"Nice, isn't it?"

"Wonderful!" She turned to him. "How is it that you can do this..." She trailed off, looking at him, feeling awkward. She couldn't remember his name. It was unlike any she had ever heard before. She looked at him apologetically.

He kindly rested a hand on her shoulder. "Lucien. Don't

worry, you will remember it in time. There is much you will learn as time goes by. You will learn about this map, about this world, even how we got here."

Hailey looked at him, confused.

"You see, you are a part of a long chain. You are part of a heritage that stretches back through time, back to the first people who arrived here on Ephryae."

"You mean the Ancestors," said Hailey.

"Yes. The people you call the Ancestors. Where do you think they came from?"

Hailey felt like she was back in school. "The stars."

"Good! And how did they get here?"

"They crashed from the sky." Hailey thought back to the *Dark Star* and how it had plummeted out of the sky after being hit by some kind of energy bolt. Thinking about it triggered something, and it finally clicked in Hailey's mind. "This isn't a cave. It's a ship!"

Lucien gave a small laugh and clapped his hands.

"Excellent! Yes, this is a fragment of what once was a great ark that traveled amongst the stars. You, my dear, are a direct descendant of one of the ship's survivors…"

"The Navigator."

Again the man smiled. "Yes, the ship's navigator." He began to walk, and Hailey joined him. The world still turned around them.

"Ah, there is so much you need to learn, but right now we don't have a lot of time."

He stopped at a door that appeared out of nowhere. He looked at her and opened it. "We'll have to start here." He motioned for her to enter.

Once inside, Hailey could see that they had stepped into a vast library. Its great red carpets led to row after row of leather-bound volumes that rested on tall wooden shelves stretching as far as the eye can see.

He stood before her and extended an arm.

"What better place to learn than in a library?" He nodded at the rows of books. "In here are the ship's logs, its information bases, and the chronicles of all of those I have helped throughout the centuries."

Hailey noticed that there were figures milling around the shelves, looking at the books.

"Who are they?" She watched them with great interest. They were all women.

"They are the Navigators who came before you."

Hailey turned to Lucien, surprised. "What are they? Ghosts?"

"No. Just afterimages. The book makes a copy of your mind to store and keep for reference."

"So there are copies of all of them?"

Lucien turned to her. "Anyone you want to talk to in particular?"

HAILEY AWOKE SUDDENLY, feeling disoriented, and she looked around to get her bearings. Her senses wouldn't tell her much; they were all too confused. All she could figure out at the moment was that she was on a soft, comfortable bed. Someone had cleaned her up. Large, blurry figures seemed to float in front of her.

"She's awake," Kyra said.

Dr. Vinkler leaned over her and looked into each of her eyes, shining a little light back and forth between them.

"How do you feel?" he asked.

Hailey's eyes snapped into focus on the doctor. She could see the concern registered on his face.

"I'm fine." She moved around a bit. She no longer felt stiff or sore, or even tired. She looked at the doctor, amazed. "I feel better than fine, I feel great!"

Captain Zordebran stepped forward out of the crowd that ringed her bed. He held his hat nervously.

"Good, so you can tell us what happened. I mean, what kind of witchcraft was that?"

"What do you mean?" Hailey looked at him, puzzled.

A voice to her left answered the question. "He means…" Hailey turned to see the sandy-colored eyes of Hadyn Winder on her. She looked down and noticed that he was also holding her hand. "When you got to the device and turned it on, we all passed out. When we woke up, all of our wounds were healed."

The hulking form of Olau stepped forward. "Look," he said, pointing to himself. There were no cuts or scars on his body as he had before. Where an eyepatch had covered a scar, there was now an eye. More startling was that hook on his left hand was gone. In its place was an actual hand. Olau opened and closed his new hand in a fist over and over again. "What kind of witchcraft is this that I could regrow my hand?"

"Was it the plague?" Kyra stood behind Hadyn. In one hand was the book, and the other held the cylinder from the cave. She extended the cylinder to Hailey, who held up her hand and shook her head.

"I don't need to see it. I know what it was. It wasn't a plague at all, more like a swarm of tiny machines that get into your blood. The Ancestors used to use them to repair human tissue and fix people. When released without instructions, they just keep multiplying in your system until your body shuts down and you die. That's what happened in Cowl's Ridge. That device in your hand gives them instructions. In this case, I must have told them to repair everything."

Olau was still opening and clenching his fist over and over.

"How do you know?" Kyra asked.

"Rachel told me about it. We talked about a lot of things actually…" Hailey stared off into space for a long moment.

Everyone in the room looked puzzled, as she recalled the conversations she had had just moments before in the library. She had learned so much in so little time. What could more time bring? Hailey blinked and shook off her contemplation of the conversations for the moment. Changing gears, she looked to Hadyn. "So what happened to the Queen and Graver? Do you have them?"

"Well, no. A whole lot happened while you were out," said Hadyn. He still held her hand and reflexively put his other behind his head to scratch.

"After you and Kyra ditched me while I was wrestling with Graver, I almost had him when the Queen shot me in the chest with the pistol you dropped. I was dying, but I guess you fixed that." He smiled weakly at her. "When I woke up, they were gone and so was their boat."

*They must have realized that the automated defenses would be up before they could get to the top,* Hailey thought.

"I found both you and Kyra passed out at the top. Kyra came around quickly, but we couldn't wake you up. We decided to bring you inside. Oddly enough, this sick bay was the only thing lit up in the whole place."

It was no accident, she knew. Hailey swung her legs around off the bed. Standing was difficult, but manageable. She felt as if she hadn't gotten out of bed for days.

"So how long have I been out?" Hailey asked Hadyn.

"Only a few hours," he said as he came around her and rested a hand on her back to help her balance.

"Long enough for us to get a good look at this place," said

Kyra, moving to her other side. "This place is huge. Large enough to sleep an army! Shall we go check it out?"

Captain Zordebran stepped in front of Hailey, blocking them from leaving the room.

"Hailey, I wasn't joking when I welcomed you to the *Dark Star*. You are one of us now. Most of us are direct descendants from the original crew of the Pirate Queen's ship, the *Revenge*. For generations we have grown up, waiting for the missing member of our crew to come back to us. We are family. *Your family*." He leaned down and placed his hands on her shoulders. "You will always have a home with us."

For a moment, Zordebran's hard features softened, and he looked Hailey in the eye. She could see his sincerity and was touched by it.

Hailey thanked him, and the captain released her. Sensing the gravity in the room, Olau shouted, "What are we doing hanging around here? We have rooms of treasure to check out!" The group gave a cheer, and they all filed out of the sick bay to explore the vast halls and floors of their prize.

The space was cavernous, and lining the walls were room after room filled with one kind of treasure or another. As in Pirate's Cove, everything seemed sterile. Not a speck of dust, nor any insect could be found, no matter how hard Dr. Vinkler searched.

Rooms full of gold, priceless furniture, and lost artworks were only the beginning of what they found.

One room held a workshop full of magic tools that defied imagination: magic mirrors, weather equipment, and machines big and small that they couldn't even begin to figure out. In the corner of the room, they found more giant balloons for their ships, several dozen pumps like the one that was on the *Dark Star*, and even plans for a new design of a flying ship designed by Rachel's father, Malcolm Feron, from Jakar. The design was extremely advanced for over 200 years ago and there were even some aspects that would have been considered really advanced now.

Hailey watched as Chloe squealed with delight at it all and flitted about the workshop like a hummingbird, going from item to item with glee.

Hailey walked about from room to room, and in each one someone seemed to find something that made them happy. Dr. Vinkler found even more medical and surgical supplies outside the fully stocked sick bay. Olau found an armory full of weapons, many of which he had never seen before. Kyra found a room full of clothes of every style and set to trying on as many as she could. The gunner master, Malik, found a room full of cannons and powder with shot of every kind. Hadyn found a room containing metal horses like the ones Hailey had seen at the colonial mansion. Zordebran stumbled upon a room full of casks of wine, rum, and other spirits piled to the ceiling. Everyone found a room of their own desires. Everyone, that is but Hailey.

She found herself walking the corridors alone, thinking about everything that had happened. At the end of the hall was a window. She leaned against it and looked, letting her thoughts swirl with the mists outside as she replayed everything in her mind. Her finding the book, being chased, losing her dad, her fight with the Queen and Graver, somehow saving the day, and then meeting the voice behind the book, Lucien.

She also thought about what they had talked about while walking Lucien's libraries in her mind. She thought about the other people she met in that library, like Rachel Feron, the first pirate queen. She also met a younger version of her mother, and her mother's twin sister, Rhiannon whom before Hailey only knew as the Veiled Queen.

The last light of day crept slowly thorough the mists, giving them a red tinge. Hailey knew that the sun was going down, and something nagged at her that it meant that there were dark days ahead. Though they celebrated victory now, the war they'd started would be long.

The Queen would never rest until she got the book back. It was too important to her plans, that much Hailey knew. Her younger self was terrifyingly twisted and cruel. Rhiannon had been looking up dark and evil things, when Hailey's mother, Rebecca, had wisely taken the book from her and sent it away. Hailey didn't know what the Queen's plans were exactly, but she did know that the Queen was looking for tools to help her control everyone as though they were her playthings. It somehow involved the Book of the Navigator. But how would a book do that? Was there something more?

Her thoughts jumped to her dad, who might have known, but he was gone. He'd valiantly given his life trying to protect her. His loss weighed enormously on her heart. Her family was completely gone now, save for Grandmother Rose.

Lucien had told her that her grandmother was alive, but how would she take the news about her son? Had she saved Grandmother Rose only to have to kill her again with grief? Grandmother Rose had lived through the disappearance of her husband with dignity and grace; would she be able to do so again, once she found out about the death of her only son?

Hailey was so lost in her thoughts she didn't hear Hadyn walk up to her.

"There you are…" He looked her over. "Heavy is the head that wears the crown?" His eyes seemed to flash with his teeth as he smiled at her.

"Yeah, sorry, I have a lot on my mind."

"Understandable. Hey, listen, Olau grabbed a couple of casks of wine and the others are bringing up the food stores from the *Virtuous*. Why don't you join us?"

"Maybe in a minute." Hailey looked away.

Getting the hint, Hadyn turned to go. "Suit yourself. How often do you get a dinner catered courtesy of the Queen herself?" He chuckled and started to turn away, but Hailey grabbed his sleeve.

"Hadyn," she said, and he turned. He seemed surprised at her grasp but still regarded her with warm affection. His eyes made her lose her train of thought for a moment. He looked back at her as if waiting.

"I wanted to thank you…for before…or saving me." Hailey stumbled over her words. She felt her face flush.

He let the moment hang between them, then Hadyn winked at her and said, "Don't mention it."

She let him go and he walked away. Down the hallway he turned and grinned over his shoulder, then said, "Join us whenever you are ready, Your Highness." He went through the door of the great hall without looking back.

She stood for a long moment contemplating the long, empty hallway. Your Highness. From what everyone was telling her, she hadn't only inherited the book from Rachel. She'd inherited her crown, and with it all the responsibilities of a leader at war. She had much to do.

Hailey had learned from her time in the book that there were other descendants of Rachel's original pirate fleet out on the far seas, hiding from the world in the mists. It was Hailey's job to bring them back into the light. To rally the pirates and resume the fight started by Rachel over two hundred years ago. This time, the stakes were even higher. The Veiled Queen was insane and willing to slaughter cities, even continents, to get whatever she wanted. Not only were she and the pirates fighting for liberty, they were fighting for their very lives. And through it all, Hailey had to rally everyone under the black flag of rebellion and lead them to victory.

Kyra poked her head out from the great room, her bright

red hair like a beacon down the otherwise plain hallway, and caught Hailey staring blankly down the hall, lost in thought.

"There you are! Come on!" She waved over to her.

Hailey had exiled herself enough. There was much to be done, but it could wait. She entered the great hall, surrounded by friends at a feast. They all cheered.

In that moment, Hailey realized she had finally found her room full of treasure in the smiling faces of her comrades in arms, pirate and merchant alike. They welcomed her with open arms and full plates, and she was glad to join them.

They sat her at the head of the table, and the captain raised a gold chalice for a toast and placed a hand on Hailey's shoulder.

"To the Pirate Queen!" he roared, and the crowd roared back the same.

Hailey looked up at the towering figure of Captain Zordebran and said, "I thought pirates chose their leaders."

He laughed and replied, "We just did."

They all drank deeply of the sweet wine, not sure if they would have a chance to celebrate tomorrow. With her aunt the Queen still out there, anything could happen. Their fight against the Crown wasn't over. They were still outmanned, outgunned, and about to be on the run, but on this day, they had won. Tonight, as they all celebrated together, they could forget their sorrows for just a little while and have a little hope for tomorrow, and that in itself was a treasure they could all enjoy.

# CODA

## THE CAPITAL CITY OF DAVOS

"What do you mean I'm not allowed to see her? I have every right! I'm the Bishop of the Church!" Jacob Graver bowled his way past the guards, threw open the great steel doors to the Queen's formal chambers, and charged in. The guards quickly followed him, hands pulling at their swords.

The Veiled Queen was sitting on a raised throne, casually reviewing the Book of the Ancients as Graver stormed his way closer to the dais.

"What's the meaning of this? Why was I barred from seeing you?"

He stopped just short of the stairs leading to her throne. The guards were almost on him; they had struggled to keep up with his long-legged strides. Their swords were raised, ready to fight.

The Queen looked up. Seeing the commotion, she raised a hand casually to the two guards and waved them off. They stopped, sheathed their swords, and stomped out of the chamber with a look of disappointment. The steel doors shut behind them with a loud bang.

Once they were alone, Rhiannon set aside the book and regarded the tall, angry man who stood below her.

"Why would I want to see you?" she spat.

Her words reverberated around the empty chamber. She leaned forward, looking at the bishop, who stood shocked and dismayed by her tone. He could feel that under her veil, her cold, dark eyes were looking down at him with rage.

She began to tick things off with her fingers. "You lost me the girl, the book, the treasure, and not to mention one of my prized ships and my most prized ports in the west! The very one you were sent to oversee! Now it is in full rebellion, and the ships that were blockading it either defected or fled. All western commerce has stopped.

"These pirates now have the means to not only defy me, but can disable one of my greatest weapons against rebellion. They may actually have enough resources to come after us and win. All because you couldn't do as I asked!"

Jacob's indignant rage fell from his face, and a look of fear gripped him. He began to lean back a little, as if physically whipped by her words.

She smiled at him frostily. "So with those little things in mind, explain to me again why I should see you."

It was the most the Queen had said to him in weeks. They had been stranded together for several days out on the ocean with no hope of rescue. They had watched the two closest Crown ships be annihilated by lightning bolts coming from the golden spire. It was only by luck that they were picked up when they were, especially since they were so far from the shipping lanes. A whaler had come across them and picked them up. She hadn't said a word to him the entire way, as they had to endure the stench of rending fat the whole two-and-a-half-week journey back to the capital city of Davos.

He twitched slightly and winced. She had a point, and it

hurt. His shoulders fell forward in supplication. He wanted nothing more than to be back in her good graces.

"I'd like the chance to make it up to you. Let me go after the girl…" he said nervously.

"No." She raised her hand, dismissing the notion, and sat back.

"But, Rhiannon…"

The Queen's eyes quickly flitted to the doors, checking to see that they were closed. She then leaned forward and pulled up her veil. She was frowning at Graver.

"Do not forget your place, Bishop Graver," she hissed at him. "You may only address me by my personal name in my bedchambers. Do not presume to be so familiar with me. Have I made myself clear?"

Graver's face fell and he looked to the floor. "Yes, Your Highness. Please forgive me."

Seeing that she had wounded the man, her long-time ally and lover, she stood, stepped down to him, and stood at his side, embracing his shoulder.

"Jacob, you have to understand, this is how things are. You knew this from the start. I couldn't have gotten as far as I have without you and your help." She rubbed his shoulder comfortingly. He turned to her and looked into her eyes. "My plan is so close to completion, and it's all because of you. You helped me with the King. Your work in establishing the new order has been magnificent, but now I need you to do something else for me."

"I want to go after the girl," he said flatly.

The Queen sighed.

"The book and the girl are someone else's concern now."

"Whose?" he said through gritted teeth.

"A knight's," she said sternly. "Not a bishop. You are far too valuable to me to put into the field of battle like that again. I have something far more important for you to do. I need you to help quell the unrest in the western colonies. Use your Church contacts to dispel any rumors about a possible rebellion."

She waited until he nodded his assent before she continued. "Good. Once you've finished with that, go to Vregora and supervise our efforts to recover the orb. We might not even need the book to reach our goals."

She took his face in her hands. "Did you hear me? You want to make it up to me? Find me that orb."

"And once we have it?" he asked.

The Queen gave him an evil grin.

"They all die."


TO BE CONTINUED

JOIN THE PIRATE CREW!

Hey You! Join our pirate crew!

Thank you so much for spending your time reading my words! If you liked what you read, could you please leave a brief review on Amazon, GoodReads, iBooks or your favorite book site? Anything helps! Reviews are not only the highest compliment you can pay to an author, they also help other readers discover and make more informed choices about finding that next great read.

If you'd like to read more about the adventures of the Pirate Queen and the other books to come find me at:
    **Blog**: www.hnklett.com/blog
    **Facebook**: www.facebook.com/hnklett
    **Twitter**: www.twitter.com/hnklett
    **Instagram**: www.instagram.com/hnklett
    **Snapchat username:** hnklett

If you would like me to notify you when the next book is released, **join my pirate crew** at www.hnklett.com/news-letter so you are one of the first to know!

# ACKNOWLEDGMENTS

Acknowledgements: The real heroes

I truly stand on the shoulders of giants, here. You have no idea how many people who helped me get this book out and the adventure started. My thanks to you all.

First off, I truly owe a debt of gratitude to my wife, Lynn. She encouraged me to take the leap of faith and really empowered me to do what I've always wanted to do. She has been and always will be my first and best reader. To my daughter, Hope, thank you for being a wonderful daughter and putting up with me spending hours at a time glued to the computer writing you a story. To my parents, thank you so much for your guidance and love.

This book had many great hands on deck getting this ship off the ground. I want to thank my fabulous editor Crystal Watanabe for all of her hard work, great advice, and putting up with my computer glitches along the way. I couldn't have worked with a better editor! My second editor, Ann Dillon who was kind enough to help me work out the finer details of the book. Jay Artale for helping layout this book, M. Wayne Miller for his incredible artwork, and Sharon Shepard, my indispensable critique partner and voice of reason. I also have to be sure and thank my small pirate army of beta readers whose input really helped to shape this book and make it the great adventure it is! Hailey, Robin, Matt, and Mark Keller, Beth Shepard, Matt Osbourne, Sophie and Caroline Strain, Sharyl Villier, Edward Fields, Fred and Susan Chappell, K.M. Weiland, Jenna Moreci, Kim Chance, Beth Rigsbee, Darlene and Jose Adams, Jon, Jennifer, Malcolm, Anna, Doug, and Leslie Black as well as the entire Downtown Fitness on Elm family.

Finally, thank you for taking the time to read this book! I hope you enjoyed it just as much as I did writing it and I hope you look for more of my works on the shelves!

All the best,

H.N. Klett

ABOUT THE AUTHOR

H.N.Klett is a writer, podcast producer, warrior poet and (possibly) a madman, who hails from Raleigh, North Carolina. A natural story teller, H.N. has been writing and telling tales since he was a little boy, inundating teachers, professors, and anyone who would listen with his poetry, plays, short stories and novels. He uses life experiences of creating and breaking things to weave stories of intrigue, fantasy, science fiction, and humor.

He has been described as a maniac armed with a pen and has created a swath of destruction in his wake. In the process of creating this book for your enjoyment, he successfully broke an unbreakable computer, shattered a shatterproof case, and annihilated several other machines much to the chagrin of his friends and loved ones. He is kept in Greensboro, North Carolina for your safety.

You can (safely) visit him at hnklett.com.